OUTLAW HIGHLANDER

A Scottish Time Travel Romance

BLANCHE DABNEY

Chapter One

✤

Lindsey glanced up at the clock on the wall. Twenty past six. The others had long gone. When the cafe shut they just took off their aprons and left. Why couldn't she do the same?

She was going to tell him. She'd had enough of being walked over. Like her mom kept reminding her, she needed to stand up for herself. If he wanted the place spotless before she went home, he could start paying her overtime.

She wiped her brow, turning to find her boss had finally put in an appearance. Richard was known for two things, trying to touch up the staff and vanishing as soon as the rush started, only returning to count the money in the till at the end of the day.

He hunched over the notes, the fluorescent lights shining off his bald patch, making him look like a human bowling ball.

"Lindsey," he said, adding the contents of the tips jar to his pile of cash. "I'm running late. You don't mind locking up for me tonight, do you?"

One more lot of tips into his pocket. That was the icing on the cake. Come on, you can do it. Stand up to him. He needs you more than you need him. "Well, actually, I was going to see my mom and I need to renew my bus pass-"

"Great. Knew you wouldn't let me down. Safe key's in the office. See you tomorrow."

"But-."

He was already gone, slapping her ass as he went, the door slamming shut before his mid-life-crisis-mobile roared into life outside.

Great. Well done. Superbly handled. You let him touch you again. And how about that for confronting him. I need a new bus pass? How about pay me for last week already? How about stop stealing our tips? Nope, you just let him walk all over you. Again.

Her hands curled into fists as anger rose up

inside her. She soon swallowed it back down. What good did it ever do to get cross about stuff like this? She'd only get fired and how likely was she to find another job? It had taken six months just to get pot washer for a perve added to her C.V. No one wanted a historian without a degree. No one wanted Lindsey MacMillan.

She glanced up at the clock again. An hour until the next bus. She might as well catch up on some reading rather than wait in the rain at the bus stop.

Retrieving her bag from the hook on the back of the staff bathroom, she dug out the book her mom had lent her and took a seat by the window, cars outside passing by in an endless blur as she settled into her book.

The rain grew heavier, slamming into the window hard enough to drown out the death rattles of the air con. She hardly noticed. She was too busy trying to work out what it was about the book her mom loved so much.

Why was Rhona MacMillan so obsessed with Tavish Sinclair? From what she could tell he was just one more medieval Highlander among many.

She had already finished the first couple of chapters in The History of the Sinclairs. Nothing so far suggested he was anything more than a murderer.

Raised in poverty, he had schmoozed through the world of the Sinclairs until he was on the verge of becoming laird, no mean feat in a time when primogeniture was everything.

Then for some reason, he threw it all away, killing a princess without a hope of getting away with it before being exiled from the clan, somehow avoiding execution. At that point, he simply disappeared from the history books.

She couldn't see anything particularly exciting about his story apart from the section on the locket. After killing the princess he stole her locket and hid it in his childhood home. No doubt his plan was to retrieve it later to sell the ruby that she kept inside.

She already knew all about the locket. That was why her mother had bought Sinclair House. The seller could hardly believe their luck when mom had offered five thousand above the asking price for a crumbling ruin that had been on the market twenty years and was sinking into the ground underneath it. Lindsey thought her mother had gone mad when she told her about her purchase.

"That was the last of your savings!"

"But the first step to finding the ruby," Rhona replied.

That was when she found out about mom's plan. She was convinced she could find the locket where everyone else had failed. Then she could pay off the mortgage that was crippling her and save a historic house from demolition.

The house purchase had been a year ago and although the renovations were progressing, there was still no sign of the priceless locket. Money was running out.

In the last couple of months, work had ground to a halt. The work had cost much more than they could afford, even with Lindsey's help. Rhona's money had long gone but she still clung onto the hope of finding the locket.

"It'll be worth a fortune," she kept saying. "Once I find it we can do up the whole place so it's exactly how it was in his time. Won't that be a fitting tribute to an innocent man?"

Lindsey didn't have the heart to mention the flaw in her mom's plan. If Tavish Sinclair was innocent of murder, as she believed, then why would he have stolen and hidden the locket?

There was a drawing of the locket filling half the page in the book in front of her. It was a sketch originally done on parchment and long faded but it gave her a good idea of how it had looked. Small, easy to hide, hard to find, the kind of thing that could easily remain hidden forever.

What would life have been like if her mom had never found out about Tavish Sinclair? Would they still be living in the tiny flat in London? Or was fate always going to bring them up to Scotland where the only work she could find was in a high street cafe that worked her too hard and paid her too little while she tried to avoid her boss's wandering hands.

It wasn't like she could afford to pick and choose from dozens of job offers. Dropping out of university when her mom got ill meant her qualifications weren't many.

She might be able to identify a piece of pottery from five hundred years ago but that was about as useful as her wood carving skills. There wasn't exactly a lot of call for a whittler in Stirling city center.

With the book back in her bag, she locked up and ran for the bus stop, making it just in time.

She dug the book back out once she was safely onboard, returning to the chapter about Tavish's trial. The writer had skill, describing it in such detail that she felt as if she were right there, watching it all unfold before her eyes.

The murdered princess was heir to the throne. King Alexander III had died in 1286, leaving his thirteen-year-old granddaughter to rule Scotland. She traveled from Norway to Scotland to marry but made the mistake of stopping at Sinclair Castle on the way. Tavish saw a chance to take the throne of the entire country and tossed her out of a castle window to fall to her death.

She could picture the trial, defiance in the accused's eyes as he raged at them all for catching him. The people watching in angry silence as he denied having anything to do with the crime.

Fingal Sinclair attempted to defend his son but there was no way of ignoring the evidence. The locket was missing, the princess had been seen going up to Tavish's room before falling to her death. It wasn't hard to work out who'd killed her.

Tavish was found guilty of course, told he was lucky the laird was merciful, he was to be banished rather than executed. The laird knew what he was doing though, banishment was a punishment worse than death in a time when it was believed outlaws could never enter heaven.

The bus reached her stop. Cramming the book

back in her bag, she headed outside into the driving rain. It was only when the bus vanished around the corner that she remembered she'd left her jacket inside.

She waved at the bus to stop but it was already long gone. "Fantastic," she said out loud, hunching her shoulders as the torrential downpour began to soak through her uniform.

By the time she made it to Sinclair House, she was freezing cold and soaking wet. Her teeth chattered as she pushed open the front door and walked down the passage to the only inhabitable room in the entire place.

Her mom sat in front of the makeshift desk, a flickering candle next to her as she hunched over the old plans of the building.

"Hi, Mom," Lindsey said, standing on the hearth, letting her clothes drip onto the enormous slab under her feet. "Electric shorted out again?"

"There's a towel behind you somewhere," Rhona said looking at her half-drowned daughter.

Lindsey dug through the boxes to find it. "How's it going?" she asked as she rubbed her hair dry, dust falling from the rough towel into her eyes.

"The bank's been on the phone again. They're running out of patience." Rhona sighed, rubbing her eyes, suddenly looking every single one of her fifty years. "I don't know, Lindsey. Maybe I shouldn't have bought this place."

"Don't say that. You've made a lot of progress."

"One room we can live in, no electricity and no money to do anything about it? Yeah, I'm quite the shrewd property developer."

"You've done a lot. All the ivy's gone. There's a staircase that's not seen the light of day for hundreds of years and now we can use it to get started on the bedrooms thanks to you. That's not nothing."

"Sadly, the bank doesn't take ivy removal in lieu of hard currency."

"Let's eat something. You'll feel better for it."

"Good idea. Lend me twenty quid and I'll go pick up a pizza."

"Toast is fine."

"You didn't get paid?"

She winced, feeling her mom's eyes boring into her, knowing what that look meant. "He's going to pay me tomorrow."

"How long's he been saying that? You've not been paid right since you started that job. He's taking you for a ride."

"I know but he promised he'd pay me

tomorrow."

"Hang on, I thought you were going with me to see the scaffolders tomorrow."

"I was but they're short staffed. I couldn't say no."

Rhona looked like she was about to say something but then she shook it away. "Never mind. I'll make us some tea."

Lindsey changed into dry clothes while her mom got the camping stove going. By the time she was done, a mug of steaming tea was ready for her.

"What is it?" Lindsey asked, seeing the way her mom was looking at her as they sat together on the fold-out chairs. "What have I done?"

"You need to stand up for yourself, Lindsey. You can't let people walk all over you your entire life."

"I know," she replied, her toes curling. "I just don't like confrontation."

"What are you going to do when you finally get a man? Let him make all the decisions because you don't want to make a fuss?"

"If men are like Richard, I'm all right without them, thanks."

"What, bald and middle age spread doesn't get you going?"

"You forgot about the dandruff."

"How does a bald man even get dandruff?"

"I've no idea but he manages it somehow."

Rhona laughed. "You'll meet a nice man soon enough. God knows, you can't spend your entire life without one. I'd had about ten by the time I was your age. You need to get out there. Go wild. Sleep with a few strangers."

Lindsey wracked her brains for a way to change the subject. The last thing she needed was to think about her mom's exploits with the opposite sex. "Any luck finding the locket?"

Rhona laughed. "All right, I get it. You don't want to hear about your mother's conquests. But you forget it was those youthful experiments that led to me having the most perfect thing in my life."

"That vacation in Belize?"

"No, you, you little grumblekin."

"I'm not perfect."

"Yes, you are."

"I've got a rubbish job with no future. I've got no money and no prospects. All I want is to have enough to help you and I can't. I can't even get us somewhere nice to stay while you fix this place. I can't do anything and hooking up with some stranger won't change that."

"Listen," Rhona said, reaching over to the desk

to pick up an envelope. "Take this."

"What is it?"

"I haven't got time for the vacation. I need to go talk to the bank. I don't want it to go to waste. You go."

"But you paid for it when you got the all clear. Besides, I've got work. I can't go."

"You can. You don't go back into that cafe until he pays you and if that oily boss of yours has anything to say about it, he can come and talk to me.

"You can take the book and finish reading it. See if there are any clues I missed about where the locket is. And you never know, you might meet some handsome Highlander who sweeps you off your feet while you're there."

"A Highlander who's staying in Iona Campbell's Loch Tay Bed and Breakfast? Presumably, a Highlander who's a fan of chintz and tiny little porcelain dolls?"

"And tartan tea towels. Don't forget them."

"Would Mrs. Campbell even let him in?"

"Only if he leaves his sword outside."

"And takes his muddy boots off."

The two of them laughed. Lindsey looked down at the envelope. It might be nice to take a vacation.

She'd worked twelve days in a row and the thought of going in again tomorrow was not an appealing one. But she had to. She had the keys.

Rhona guessed what she was thinking. "Iona is already expecting you. I rang her this morning. I'll drop the keys off for you, might even be able to pick your pay up while I'm at it. It'll be here when you get back. Go and relax for a couple of days. Fall in love, drink lots of tea, go swimming in the loch. Not necessarily in that order."

"I can't swim, remember."

"Then go rowing on the loch. See if there's some Highlander up there with a huge-"

"Mom!"

"Wallet. I was going to say wallet. What? Why are you looking at me like that?"

The next evening Lindsey settled into the lounge of the Bed and Breakfast, picking up the photos of Tavish's house that had fallen out of the book. They'd taken them with the old Polaroid camera, cramming them into the dust jacket of the book before forgetting about them.

She sat curled up in the chair by the window,

reading her mom's book with the water of the loch lapping at the shore just a few feet away outside. As she turned the page the photos fell out.

Mrs. Campbell shuffled in, carrying a tray of tea things. Lindsey nodded to her, shoving the photos into the pocket of her jeans.

"Dinnae let it go cold," she said as she walked in.

"Thank you," Lindsey replied, putting the book down on the little table beside the chair.

"History o' the Sinclairs," Mrs. Campbell said, nodding toward the cover. "Good book. Was an awfa shame what happened to that wee princess. Tavish must have been a wicked brute to kill such an innocent girl."

"My mom says he didn't do it."

"Does she indeed? She must ken something I dinnae. If it wasnae for him slaughtering wee Margaret we'd never have gone tae war? Does she ken that?"

Lindsey frowned. "I don't think I've reached that bit yet."

"When Margaret was killed, two men fought over who should be king. There was John Balliol and Robert the Bruce. They bickered so long Edward came up from England to choose for them.

Only he'd not dae it until they bowed down tae him first. Balliol would and the Bruce wouldnae. So Balliol gets the throne and the Bruce rallies anyone who wouldnae bow tae the English.

"Five years later the whole country is at war, half beside Bruce and half with Balliol and thousands dead all because Tavish wanted tae be laird and that wee lassie got in his way. The man was, and I dinnae like to use the word, scum. Only way tae describe one such as he. And I hear Rhona went and bought his house. Why would she want to do something so daft?"

"She heard it was going to be demolished and she-"

Mrs. Campbell interrupted her. "Belonged to a killer. Demolition is what it deserves." Her look darkened for a moment before her smile returned. "Oh look, the sun's out. You should go rowing, get some air intae your lungs."

"I'm happy reading, thanks."

"Take the book with you."

"I'd love to but I can't swim. What if I fall out?"

"Just stay near the shore. It's shallow enough to walk back in if you capsize."

"But my tea, it'll get cold."

"Och, dinnae worry. I'll make a fresh batch.

You never ken how long the sun might stay out up here. Make the most of it while you can. You get out on the water. Your ma always loved rowing out there. I know you'll love it tae."

Lindsey wanted to refuse but couldn't bear hurting the old woman's feelings. Mrs. Campbell led her out of the guesthouse and down to the boat.

Lindsey glanced along the shore. A man was standing about twenty feet away, looking out at the loch, mist swirling around his ankles. He had a red tartan baldric across his bare chest and looked every inch the medieval Highlander in black trousers that clung to him, spear in his hand pointed toward the water.

"Who's that?" Lindsey asked. "He looks like he's just walked off the set of Outlaw King."

"I cannae see anyone," Mrs. Campbell replied, looking over the top of her glasses. "Though I've been meaning to get another eye test."

Lindsey looked again but there was no one there. Just the mist growing thicker despite the sun high in the sky. "I could have sworn I saw-"

Mrs. Campbell thrust the book into her hands, distracting her. "Here. Take it with ye. Best place to read about the Highlands is in the middle of Loch Tay."

"I thought you said to stay near the shore."

"You enjoy yourself out there."

With a push from Mrs. Campbell, the rowing boat began to ease out onto the water, rocking slightly on the gentle waves. Lindsey waved back at her host as she was swallowed up by the mist.

Silence fell. Taking hold of the oars, she began to row. A breeze blew the mist away and then she was able to see the rolling green hillsides around the loch. The water grew still as a millpond.

There was no risk of her falling out. She wondered why she'd been so worried. A deep sense of contentment came to her as she lay back with the book on her chest and began to read.

She soon lost herself in the detailed description of the murder of Princess Margaret who had only gone to visit Tavish in his chamber in the north tower of the castle. She was there to reject his proposal of marriage, tell him she was betrothed to Edward Caernarvon.

He grabbed her in a rage, snatching the locket from around her neck before hurling her from the window. She could picture it, the princess falling screaming to her death. Tavish thinking he'd assured himself of the crown by getting rid of the only heir.

The only problem was none of it made sense. How would killing her help him get the throne? He wasn't from a noble background. He had no army to back him. He wasn't even a laird. Why would anyone accept him saying he should be king?

She read the chapter again, hoping to spot something she might have missed. A breeze picked up but she didn't notice, she was too engrossed in the book. The breeze pushed the boat slowly away from the shore as the mist began to swirl around it again, blocking her view of the land.

By the time Lindsey realized what was happening, she was in the middle of the loch. The mist parted once more and she saw the shore far away but didn't recognize the view. The trees were gone, the hillside bare. Where was the Bed and Breakfast?

"Keep calm," she told herself as the breeze stiffened into a strong wind that rocked the boat from side to side. "Just get back to the shore and then you can work out where you are."

She started to row but it was hard. Whichever way she went the wind seemed to be against her, pushing her back toward the middle of the loch. Her arms ached from the effort as she shoved the oars down into the water again and again.

Out of nowhere there came a scraping sound

somewhere under the boat. She fell back with a thump. Then something smacked into the hull.

Leaning over, she caught a glimpse of a jagged rock wedged into the side near the oar. As she tried to dislodge it a sudden gust blew, catching her off-guard. Before she could right herself, she tipped forward and fell headfirst into the water.

It was freezing, the icy cold making her gasp as she plunged down into the dark. She swallowed a lungful of water and that sent her into a blind panic. Thrashing her limbs, she managed to surface for long enough to see a figure on the shore.

She tried to wave for help, but she sank almost at once. Bobbing back up, there was no time to take another breath before she went under again, lungs burning, body screaming for air.

Kicking her legs, she prayed she could get onto the rock that was sticking out of the water, but it seemed to have vanished. She could feel nothing, see only darkness. She tried to push for the surface, but it got further away and then she slowly began to sink down toward the bottom of the loch.

This is it, she thought in the midst of her panic. This is how I'm going to die.

Chapter Two

T avish dragged the woman's body out of
the water and lay it down on the heather.
He knelt beside her and placed a hand
on her chest. Was she dead?

All of a sudden, her eyes opened. She coughed
up a fountain of water, slapping his hand away
from her a moment later. "Who are you?"
she asked.

"Ye need tae take those clothes off, lass," he
said. He was surprised by the sound of his own
voice. It had been many years since he'd spoken to
anyone.

"Keep away from me," she snapped, still scut-
tling away.

He sighed, shaking his head. "Keep going,

English. You'll be passed out in under a minute and I'll just wait 'til then tae get them things off you, shall I?"

"Where am I?" Her teeth were chattering and the last of the color was draining from her face. She'd be gone soon.

"On the side o' Loch Tay and aboot to die o' the cauld."

"Stay away from me. What am I doing here?" Her eyes rolled into the back of her head and she fell heavily on her back, moving no more.

Tavish looked up at the sky. "Ah was happy enough on ma own." God had a dark sense of humour at times, it seemed. "Why'd you send me her?"

He walked over to her as she jerked awake again. She pointed a wild finger at him. "You stay away from me or I'll scream."

"Go ahead, there's none but me and the coneys tae hear ye."

"Mrs. Campbell will hear me. I recognize this bit of shore. She's just around the corner. Probably calling the police already."

"Good. Maybe your Mrs. Campbell can talk some sense into ye before you drop deed o' the cauld."

"What are you talking about?"

He sighed. Could she be that ignorant of the danger? "You need to get them off ye before the chill kills ye."

She glanced out at the loch. "Where's my boat?"

"About thirty feet down by noo. It fell apart when you hit yon rock."

"The rock?" She paused. "I remember. I hit a rock and I fell out. I was drowning. Then-"

"Then ah dragged you out. Ah wouldnae have bothered if I'd known you'd be like this."

"You…you saved me?"

He nodded.

"But why?"

"Are we going to blether all day or dae ye want tae stay alive? Get them wet things off noo."

She was shivering uncontrollably as she stood there, her arms wrapped around her chest. "I'm not undressing in front of you."

He wiped the water from his face with his palm, trying to keep calm. "This way." He picked up his fishing rod and headed home. He didn't bother to look behind him. She'd follow if she wanted to live.

"Where are we going?" Her voice a few feet back.

She was following him then. He was glad. He had enough deaths on his conscience. There was no need to add another one.

"To ma house," he said, climbing up a steep slope and then down the other side. His self-made hut sat buried amongst gnarled old trees, barely visible unless you knew where to look.

He stopped in front of it. "Ah've got some things you can change intae for noo."

She didn't answer. She was barely conscious. Her skin was so white it was almost blue. She had minutes at most before it would be too late.

"Inside and get changed noo or ah'll tear them things off you ma self."

She scrambled away from him, fear flaring in her eyes. In her rush to get inside she banged her head on the top of the doorframe, staggering back. He caught her before she could fall, helping her upright.

She looked at his hand on her shoulder, the other one on her waist, a dazed look across her face. He let go at once. No doubt she'd heard the stories about him and was terrified of what he might do. Was it worth correcting her? Probably not. No one ever believed the truth. Why should she be any different?

"The fire's lit," he said as she vanished inside. "Top it up with some of the peat while you're in there."

He shoved the door closed before leaving her to it, walking over to sit on the worn oak stump. He dug the knife out from his pocket. Soaked by the loch, it was already so rusty the water could do no more damage. Picking up the end of the fishing rod, he began to carve. One day he would carve a decent hook. How long had it been since he'd been able to get hold of proper metal?

He looked across at the line of stones in the grass in front of him. The nearest ones were almost swallowed by weeds. The more recent was scored with upright lines, a tally of weeks. He tried to add them up but he soon lost count. There was at least eight years worth, maybe ten. A long time to spend in exile.

The first year, he'd almost gone mad. All he could think about was the injustice of it all, being accused and convicted of a crime he didn't commit, the entire clan despising him. Told to be thankful for banishment instead of execution.

He thought about that and managed a bitter smile. The laird knew exactly what he was doing. Banishment meant living with knowing his father was in the dungeon. Execution meant release from the pain of the injustice. He'd have taken execution any day given the choice. But he wasn't given the choice.

He'd come to terms with it over time. He thought about suicide often in the first days and weeks but something always stopped him. A whispering voice that said one day something would come along that he could use to free his father.

He learned to survive while he waited. There was just him and his hidden corner of the world. In the last couple of years, he'd almost begun to enjoy it.

So why had he decided to help her? He retraced his steps. He'd been sitting by the shore looking out at the water, waiting for a bite. It had been three days since he'd caught a fish, the last of his knives too blunt to carve decent hooks anymore.

He was hungry and worn out, having not slept yet again.

Then she just appeared out of the mist in the middle of the loch. He must have been more tired than he thought. He hadn't seen her row out there but all of a sudden there she was, falling into the water, her boat splitting apart around her.

He was diving in before he even knew he was doing it.

The time in exile had honed his waistline which helped with the rescue. He'd gone from fairly strong as laird in waiting to nothing but muscle, not a trace of fat on him.

His arms had swelled beyond all recognition, the result of years of chopping and carrying wood to keep warm at night. His limbs pushed effortlessly through the water and he reached the spot where she'd gone under in less than a minute.

Taking a deep breath, he dived down, not knowing if he was too late. The light above the surface penetrated no more than a couple of feet. She was nowhere to be seen. He came up, took another breath, and then went under again, groping in the murk.

Just when he was sure he was too late, his finger-tips caught something. He grabbed hold and didn't let go. It was her hand. He hauled her up to the surface, dragging her with him as he kicked back for the shore, one arm hooked under her armpit, holding her tight as he lay on his back, his other arm sweeping through the waves.

It took no more than a couple of minutes to get her to dry land. He dragged her unconscious body over the silty shoreline to the heather, laying her down and moving quickly to get her wet things off. He was certain he was too late, that she was dead or dying, that it was all a pointless endeavor.

Then she was fighting him off even while he tried to save her. He smiled as he thought of it. He was trying to save her life and she was so stubborn she tried to stop him. She had some spirit, he had to give her that.

As he waited for her to change, he found himself thinking about her clothes. They were like nothing he'd ever seen on a woman before. She wore blue hose of the coarsest fabric that clung to her skin in the most scandalous manner. Her boots were of several colors, all held together by loops of thick white string.

Her top half was almost naked, her arms uncovered, her neck on show, the only clothing a single chemise of floral cloth. The whole ensemble was utterly bizarre but also intriguing. She had to be a jongleur. It was the only possible explanation.

She'd had long enough. He walked over to the hut in time to hear a thud.

"Help, I can't get the door open,"

Her accent intrigued him as much as her

clothes. What was an English lass doing so far north of the border?

"Haud on," he said, grabbing the door and yanking it open, the wood groaning in protest. Setting it down, he walked inside.

"Don't mind me," she said.

"Wait outside," he said, pulling his hose from his legs. Did she think she was the only one to get wet from their swim?

He glanced behind him, but she was nowhere to be seen. Good. Hopefully, she'd gone back to wherever she came from.

A thought occurred to him a second later. What if she told someone where he was? His peace would be shattered by those who had bayed for his blood during the trial, coming and forcing him to fight, to kill. He was done with killing.

He frantically pulled on the only dry pair of hose he had left. With that done he ran outside, ready to hunt her down and stop her from blabbing.

What he saw startled him. She hadn't run off. She was sitting on the stump of wood, the sunlight shining on her slowly drying hair. She looked like an angel. An angel who was using his spare knife to carve a hook into the end of his fishing spear.

He stood in the doorway and looked at her for a

while. She hadn't noticed him. He took in the view. The hose she had borrowed, the length of tartan cloth she'd wrapped around her chest in lieu of a dress.

Her hair was dark, cascading over her shoulders. He had never seen a woman with hair uncovered like that. Even the peasants wore basic coifs. She didn't seem the least bit concerned that she'd lost her hat in the water. She was humming to herself as she worked.

She glanced up at him and he looked away, not wanting to be caught spying on her. "That should work better now," she said, holding out the spear.

He doubted it. Then he examined the hook. "How did ye do that?"

"How did I do what?"

"'Tis sharp as steel and done wi' a blunt knife. How?"

She shrugged. "It's not tricky if you know what you're doing."

For a moment Tavish didn't know what to say. He examined the fishing rod again. "I must try it out. Wait there."

"I'm not going anywhere."

He headed back to the loch. Standing on the shore, he peeled off the hose from his legs before edging slowly out into the water. He kept going until he reached the deep pool where the fish were most often found. He stood perfectly still when he got there, the only sound that of the curlews in the distance. There was not a breath of wind in the air.

This was his favorite time. When there was nothing but him and the Highlands. He felt part of the land and the loch. It was at moments like that he forgot about his past. He needed no one. Just the Highlands.

He didn't move, waiting patiently, ignoring the growling of his stomach after so long without food. To his surprise trout began to circle around his ankles within minutes. He held the rod ready, taking a steady breath before thrusting down at lightning speed, spearing a fish and bringing it upward into the air.

It fought briefly to free itself from the hook before succumbing. He smiled to himself. The spear had worked perfectly. He'd have to get her to show him how she'd done it with such a blunt knife.

He dressed quickly. Then, with the fish in one hand and the rod in the other, he headed back, finding her gone from the stump. How could he have been so stupid? She just wanted him out of the way so she could make a run for it. Tell them all where he was hiding out.

He was kicking himself for his stupidity when he heard her humming inside the hut. He stuck his head in the door and marveled at what she'd done while he'd been away.

There had originally been a window when he'd first put the place together but he'd wedged a log in the sill during the last winter and never bothered removing it. She'd taken out the log to use as a second stool by the fireside.

She was sitting on the log with her feet outstretched toward the fire, light streaming in through the window. There was even a posy of flowers by the hearth, the scent of the flowers making the whole place smell like a meadow.

"You managed to catch a fish," she said with a smile, nodding toward his hand.

"Aye, and you managed to go rummaging while I was away. If you're looking for Princess Margaret's locket you'll nay find it in there."

"I wasn't looking for anything. I just wanted something to sit on while I get warm. Where do you sit?"

"The floor." He gutted the fish before grabbing a spike from the hearth, skewering the trout. He set the spike over the flames and left the carcass to spit down into the burning peat, the smell of cooking fish soon overpowering the scent of the flowers.

"Are ye warm enough?" he asked.

"Yes, thank you," she said, getting to her feet.

"Why did ye no swim?"

"Huh? Oh, in the loch? I can't swim?"

"Ye cannae swim and yet ye went oot in the middle of a loch? Jings, ye must be daft in the heed."

"I wasn't planning to fall out," she said, pouting like a child. "I didn't realize I'd drifted so far, that was all."

"Aye, well, ye should be more careful next time."

"There's not going to be a next time. I'm going home tomorrow."

"Back tae England?"

"Yes, why? Why say it like that?"

"Because it takes a brave soul tae travel so far north o' the border when we're on the verge of going tae war."

"War? Who with?"

"The English of course." He leaned toward the fire, rotating the fish on its makeshift spit.

"Listen, there might be some grumbles between

England and Scotland over soccer from time to time but this is first I've heard of war."

He lifted the fish from the fire. "Ah might be wrong. It's been a long time since I heard news of anything. Ready to sup?"

He sliced the fish into thick chunks, passing the first handful to her.

She looked at it for a moment before starting to eat. "You know," she said after swallowing, "you've got this hunter-gatherer thing down pat, haven't you? What was it, corporate life got too much for you, wanted to get back to basics?"

"Will ye just eat?"

His stomach was glad of the fish. As he ate, he glanced at her again. She was looking into the fire, but she turned to match his gaze. He held her eyes for a second before looking away.

The rest of the meal was eaten in silence. When he was done, he wiped the grease from his hands onto his hose.

"You really are an animal, aren't you?" she said, rising to her feet and walking outside.

"Where are ye going?"

He got his answer when he saw her neatly wiping her own hands on the grass outside. She returned to the doorway.

"That was lovely, thank you. I've never eaten a meal quite like it. If you're passing by the guesthouse, you should call in, have something cooked in an oven for once. You might like it."

"Ye cannae go." He was up in under a second, striding outside and getting a hand to her shoulder, spinning her around to look at him.

She looked down at his hand, then up at him as it lingered there. "Why can't I go?"

He realized, letting go a second later. "You're English and you're on Sinclair land. The first patrol tae see you will have you skewered like that fish."

"Not this again. Look, I need to get back. It's been lovely…sorry, what was your name?"

"Tavish."

"Tavish what?"

"It was Sinclair before they booted me out on me arse. Now it's just Tavish."

She frowned before smiling. He was surprised by how pretty she looked when she smiled, her eyes lighting up. "Very funny. What's your real name?"

"Tavish Sinclair."

"You're Tavish Sinclair? As in, the Tavish Sinclair. And I suppose this is what, 1290? 1300?"

"It were 1290 when ah were banished. I suppose it must be around 1300 now, give or take."

The smile faded from her lips. "You're telling me this is the year 1300?"

"Aye."

"Oh, God. You're being serious. You really think it's 1300, don't you?" She started backing away from him, looking at him like he was a wild animal.

"Where are ye going? Ah said ye cannae go."

"Yes, I can. You're insane."

She turned and ran, sprinting into the distance.

For a moment he was too surprised to react. Then he thought about her blabbing to the Sinclairs about where he was holed up.

He thought about having to move again just when he was finally finding some peace. A moment later he was sprinting out of the hut and hunting her down.

Chapter Three

Lindsey didn't hear him coming until it was too late. All she heard was her own heavy breathing. She had to hold the tartan in place across her chest as the knot she'd tied began to come loose.

It only needed to hold until she got back to Mrs. Campbell's. Then she could get changed and forget about all this. Forget about insane Scotsmen who thought it was the middle ages.

As if he was Tavish Sinclair? The very idea would be funny if she weren't so scared. She'd realized he was serious when he looked into her eyes and told her his name. He really thought he was the outlaw Highlander who'd lived seven hundred years earlier.

At that moment when he looked at her, she knew she'd made a mistake. She was alone with a dangerously unstable individual and she was too far from the guesthouse to summon help. Even if she'd screamed, by the time help came it would have been too late for her.

She ran through a copse of trees and then out the other side. The hillside was familiar. This was where the taxi had brought her down the worn track to the guesthouse when she first arrived. Another corner and past that ridge and it would be right in front of her. She put on a fresh burst of speed, panicking that he might be trying to follow her.

Scrambling up the ridge, she stumbled over the top, more falling than running down the far side. In her effort to keep her balance she stared down at her feet, trying to avoid the loose stones rolling down with her.

She skidded to a halt at the bottom of the slope. "Back at last," she said, looking up before falling silent. She almost fell again, this time from surprise. The hill was there just like before, the groove of the dried-up stream was still there only now water was flowing from it into the loch to her left.

Where was the guesthouse? The hillside was

there, the flat ground leading to the loch. She was definitely in the right place but there was no building, just tufts of deep green grass and occasional patches of thistles.

"But where is it?" she said out loud, taking a step forward as if the guesthouse might appear from nowhere. "I must be in the wrong place."

She walked to the top of the next ridge but there was nothing but wilderness down the far side. She mashed her fingers together without noticing what she was doing, her eyes darting from left to right. "It must be here somewhere. Please don't tell me I'm lost."

Spinning around, she let out a cry. On the top of the ridge, the Highlander was standing, looking every inch like Tavish Sinclair had been described in the book.

The wind blew the tartan on his muscular chest, his hair moving too in the breeze. The black hose on his legs could barely contain his quads, they looked like they might rip through at any point. He wasn't even breathing heavily. How had he run so fast after her without working up a sweat?

He had his hands on his hips, staring down at her in silence. "You stay away from me," she snapped, pointing up at him. "I've got enough problems without you chasing after me. Where's the guesthouse?"

"What guesthouse?"

"Mrs. Campbell's. It was right here, I swear it."

"Ah know this loch like the back o' me hand. There's nay been a building here 'til ah built ma hoose back there."

Something whispered to Lindsey. *You're in the past.* She ignored the voice, shaking her head as she looked around again. "It has to be here. This is Loch Tay, right?"

"Aye, lass." He walked slowly down the hillside toward her, a strange look on his face.

"Then where's Mrs. Campbell's?"

"There's nae building until you get tae Castle Sinclair a fair stretch o' miles that way." He pointed up the hillside away from the loch.

"There's about three villages between here and there."

The anger had gone from his face, his eyes wider, a flicker of a smile on his lips. "You mustae hit yon heed pretty hard when you fell out your boot."

"I hit my head? You think you're Tavish Sinclair, the princess murdering Highlander." She saw the look on his face. "Oh, yes. I know all about that."

The smile had gone, his eyes flaring with anger. "I didnae kill her."

The look sent Lindsey backward. The glare was impossible to withstand. "You're not him. You can't be him."

His voice grew quiet, far colder than before. "Ah am Tavish Sinclair. My father is Fingal Sinclair and if he lives, he rots in a dungeon tae this day. I lived in Castle Sinclair until the day o' ma trial."

"You really believe that, don't you? That you're him."

"Why would ah lie about such a thing?"

"You killed Princess Margaret of Norway?"

"Ah didnae kill her."

"This must be a dream. It has to be."

"You're no dreaming, lass."

"I am. How else can I be talking to Tavish Sinclair next to a vanished guesthouse? Wait, what year did you say it was? 1290?"

"1300."

She spoke more to herself than him. "I've gone back in time."

"What?"

"If I'm not dreaming and you really are Tavish Sinclair, then I've gone back in time."

"What are ye blethering about?"

She grabbed hold of his arms. "I've gone back in time. Don't you get it? It must have been the mist. Or when I fell out of the boat. That's why the guesthouse isn't here. It hasn't been built yet. Oh, my goodness. You really are Tavish Sinclair. This is insane."

She moved away, running her hand through her hair. "I've gone back in time." A thought struck her. She fell to the ground, landing heavily on the grass.

"How do I get back?" she said, laying on her back and staring up at the sky. "I'm stuck here forever."

A shadow fell across the sky. Tavish was standing blocking out the light, looking down at her. He was nothing more than a silhouette with the sun behind him. "This isnae your time, is it?"

"You got that right." She closed her eyes. "I'm stuck in 1300 with Tavish Sinclair. You know, it's funny. My mom would kill to be in my place right now."

"Why's that?"

"She loves you."

His brow furrowed. "How does she ken me?"

"Never mind. It's not worth explaining."

"When are ye from?"

"I'm not born until about seven hundred years from now. Which is a bit weird when you think about it like that."

"Ah might be able to help you get back."

She shot upright. "What? You can get me back to my own time?"

"Not me. The island."

"How?"

"We'll swim across."

"I can't swim."

"Ah."

"Any idea where I could get a boat?"

He held her gaze for a moment before answering. Should he tell her about his secret? His one memorial to his mother, the boat he'd carved and hidden away and vowed never to use, ready for her journey across the river to the everlasting sea. He had no reason to share it with her.

"Aye," he said at last.

The walk seemed to take forever. By the end of it, Lindsey's feet were sore. She feared taking her sneakers off. She felt sure there was blood down there from burst blisters. His pace had been relentless from the moment they set off up the mountainside. She was soon lost as they moved along the ridge and then down into a valley filled with lush heather.

The entire time they walked, she saw no one. The sun was setting by the time they stopped. She had fallen far behind and was limping to try and keep up when he glanced behind him.

"Rest," he said, coming back to her.

"I'm fine. I thought you said this boat wasn't far away."

"It's another mile but I dinnae ken whether it will still be there."

Lindsey looked behind her. All day to get from one side of the loch to the other. It would have been no more than an hour by car. She'd no idea it could take so long to walk somewhere when there were no paths to follow.

Occasionally they came across rabbit trails but most of the time she had to push her aching legs through thick bushes of heather that hid numerous holes in the earth below.

Twice she'd fallen, almost twisting her ankle. Both times he'd helped her up without a word. Then he was striding off again like he was a ghost, the terrain not slowing him for a moment.

Was he a ghost? She found herself thinking as she walked. There was still the slim chance she was dreaming all this though that seemed increasingly unlikely. He had lived and died all those years ago and yet there he was in front of her, marching on without a care in the world.

That wasn't true. He had flashed such rage about the death of the princess that she vowed not to bring the subject up again. Instead, she focused on where she was going, trying to ignore the hunger growing inside her and the increasing pain in her feet.

When he noticed her limping and insisted they rest, she didn't refuse the invitation, stretching out on the grass, taking deep breaths and refusing to think about what would happen if this didn't work.

He sat beside her, staring into the distance and saying nothing. She took the chance to examine him better. How did he compare to what the history books had said?

He was different from how she'd imagined him, she knew that for sure. She'd pictured a cruel murderer laughing over the corpse of his victim, arrogance, and entitlement written across his face. The reality was very different.

There was pain behind his eyes, one she had noticed early on despite his refusal to express much in the way of emotion. His hair was long, his skin darkened by a life lived in the sun. She took in the muscles on his arms, the way he sat perfectly still, his legs still looking like they might burst out of the hose at any moment.

"Ready?" he asked, looking across at her. "If we get a move on, we should make it by dark." He got to his feet and held a hand down to help her up.

"I'm ready," she said, taking the proffered hand. He lifted her upright in a second. She took a step and then winced, pain coursing through her foot.

"Are ye all right, lass?"

"I'm fine."

He nodded before setting off. She followed, doing her best to ignore the pain.

"What happens when we find the boat?" she called after him.

He slowed his pace until he was beside her. "We take you to the island and see if the rumors are true."

"What rumors?"

"All ah know is that the well on the island has powers beyond man's ken. The druid knows more about it than ah do."

"So, it might not work?"

He didn't answer. She tried not to think about what she'd do if it didn't work, if she was forever stuck in this time. Mom would lose the house and would never know what happened to her daughter. It had to work. She had to believe it would work.

It took another hour to get down to the lochside. When they arrived, Tavish vanished into the undergrowth, dragging out a moss-covered rowing boat.

"How long's that been there?" she asked.

"Ah found it the first year ah was here."

"Why haven't you used it?"

He didn't answer, pushing the boat toward the water before stopping. "Do ye wantae eat before you go?"

She nodded in response. "I'm starving."

"Get a fire going. I'll trap us some rabbits. We passed a warren back there."

"Get a fire going? What with?"

He muttered something under his breath, already turning away.

"What?" She tried again. "What did you say?"

"Find some kindling. Ah'll do the rest."

He headed back up the hillside leaving Lindsey alone. She walked over to the boat and examined it. Would it survive a trip to the island? The last thing she wanted was to fall out and end up soaking wet for the second time in one day.

She prodded the wooden planks which creaked in response. Don't think about it, she told herself, turning away to search for firewood.

By the time Tavish got back the light had almost died. She had a decent sized pile of wood ready for him when he walked down the hillside. "Two rabbits," she said as he joined her by the woodpile. "You provide quite a feast."

"We might have tae wait until morning," he said, looking at the sky, the last of the light fading below the horizon. "To row across." He knelt by the fire and began tearing shreds of bark to make kindling.

"Oh. Can't we do it in the dark?"

"Not if we want tae find the island." He began scraping a flint toward the kindling, sparks shooting across to the scraps of bark.

"It can't be that hard can it?"

"Big loch, wee island. Eat. Sleep. Then leave."

She looked at the fire which was already catching, heat thawing her chilled hands. Her stomach rumbled loudly.

She turned away as he effortlessly skinned and prepared the rabbits. She was used to her meat drizzled in oil, not scraped from the skin.

When she looked back again, he was using a long stick from the woodpile as a spit. Soon the air was filled with the smell of roasting meat. Lindsey's stomach growled all the louder.

"You're going back tae your time?" Tavish asked out of nowhere.

Lindsey glanced up to see him looking down at the fire, poking the flames back into life.

"Hopefully. Wait until I tell my mom I met you. She'll never believe me."

"Why does she care?"

"My mom loves you. She swears you didn't do it."

"Didnae dae what?"

"Kill the princess. She says you were innocent."

"What do you ken?"

"I'm not sure."

His voice was still a bear's growl but somehow seemed softer. "She's right, you ken? Ah didnae do it."

Chapter Four

❧

While Lindsey slept soundly, Tavish dreamed of the day it all went wrong for him. Lilias brought him flowers. By the end of the day he was on trial for murder.

He was fishing in his favorite spot, sitting beside the water and staring out at the perfect stillness. The only place he could get away from giving orders and resolving disputes, dealing with all the stresses of clan life.

The surface reflected the blue sky, a single cloud slowly drifting by, soon to vanish behind the distant mountains.

The peaks were topped with snow. Even at the height of summer, some peaks never thawed. He recalled the first time his father took him up there. He'd been eight years old when plague struck.

For six months they lived off the land away from the village, waiting to see if the symptoms emerged. Only when spring turned into summer did his father decide they were safe. Somehow, they had survived when the rest of the village had perished. All his fault. A guilt he would bear to his death.

"We're fortunate," his father told him when he asked if they could go home. "We have been given a chance for a fresh start. We shall travel to Castle Sinclair. Fortunes are made there, my boy. One day you'll be laird."

Tavish smiled but he knew it was nonsense. The lordship passed from father to first son, never to a distant relative raised in poverty and unknown to any at the castle. Still, what harm in letting his father dream?

First, they climbed the mountain, Fingal offering thanks to God from the highest peak for saving his son from the ravages of illness that regularly swept the Highlands. When he was done, the two of them descended the steep slopes to the worn track that led east to the castle.

The mountains watched over him and his father

as they settled into life at the castle. His father's skills as a blacksmith were put to good use while Tavish was taken into the laird's household, taught the manners of a squire.

When they saw how good his skills were with a sword, he went from potential squire to potential knight. By the time he was fifteen he was being tipped for future laird, having made himself indispensable during several skirmishes with rival clans. Then it all went wrong. All because of one twelve-year-old girl and her flowers.

She brought them back from the island. "Orange heather," Lilias said, almost stumbling out of the boat when it scraped the bottom of the loch. She ran up the shore to him, flowers held out in front of her. "I got them for you."

Tavish patted the ground next to him. He needed to do this gently but tact had never been his strongest characteristic. "Ye know you're no supposed tae row out there alone. What if you'd fallen in?"

"Then you would have come and saved me. It would have been magical."

"I didn't even know you were there. Ye would be deed and bloated in the water."

"You would have saved me." She looked up at

him with the utterly certain conviction of hero worship. He never knew why she'd latched onto him. For the last year, she'd been bringing him more and more flowers, sweetmeats from the kitchen, even fetching water from the well for him while he sweated in sword practice. No matter how many times he sent her away she kept coming back.

He got to his feet. It was time to end this nonsense once and for all. "Take those flowers tae Margaret."

"Are you going to marry her?"

Tavish shook his head. "Whatever gave ye that foolish idea?"

"I saw the way she was looking at you when she arrived."

"I'm a blacksmith's son. She's a princess."

"So? You're going to be laird one day. Everyone's saying it. Then you could be king and her your queen."

"It's not that simple, Lilias. Margaret is going to marry Edward Caernarvon."

"So, who are you going to marry?"

"I'm not going tae marry anyone."

"You could marry me. Hey, where's your locket gone?"

Tavish felt for his neck, his hand touching nothing. He couldn't tell her that Margaret had snatched it from him that morning. How could he tell anyone the heir to the throne was a thief?

"I must have lost it."

"You gave it to her as a keepsake. I knew it. You love her, not me." She was on her feet in a shot. "I see how you're looking at me. You think I'm just a stupid child who doesn't know how the world works. You're going to marry the stupid princess and you should have just said so."

She stormed off up the beach. "Lilias," he shouted after her.

She ignored him, breaking into a run. He swore to himself. There would be no peace to fishing anymore. His father would come and berate him for not keeping the laird's favourite niece onside.

He headed back. By the time he made it to the castle she'd disappeared. He found the place alive with activity, the coming of the heir to the throne had thrown the entire castle into turmoil.

Fresh rushes had been laid across the courtyard, there were bouquets everywhere. The forge had been damped down for the first time in months. It was strange walking past it without feeling heat coming from the flames.

He stayed away from the great hall. Margaret

had been set up in there with her retinue, enter-
tained by the laird and his musicians. The sound of
a lyre echoed from the windows, soon lost among
the noise of conversation and laughter.

He didn't want to see Margaret, not after what
had happened that morning. He'd found her in his
chamber, rummaging through his things. His father
was nowhere to be seen. He wasn't sure of the
etiquette of asking a future queen what she thought
she was doing.

He coughed politely and she turned to face him.

"I sneaked away," she said. "I wanted to
see you."

"Me?" He got his first proper look at the future
queen. She was little older than Lilias, thin nose,
bony cheeks, ice white hair. She looked far more
Nordic than Highland. She had a curl to her smile
that suggested she was terribly amused by everything she saw, alongside being perfectly at home
telling others what to do.

"You. I saw you when I arrived, sweating at
the forge, that chest of yours glistening in the
light. I wanted to see if you looked as handsome
up close and you do. What's that around your
neck?" She took a step toward him, pointing at
the locket.

He pulled it over his head, passing it to her. "It belonged to my mother."

"I like it. I shall have it. Here, you may have mine in return."

"I dinnae want yours-"

"Are you refusing a gift from your future queen?" She gave him a look that said execution was a click of the fingers away.

"No, your highness."

"Good." She tucked his locket into a fold of her dress, turning back to look out of the window once again. "They wish me to marry Edward. What do you think would happen if I told them I had married a blacksmith's boy? Wouldn't that be so funny?"

Tavish shook his head, not that she could see it. There would be war. Edward would attack the clan and hundreds would die. It would be very far from funny.

She looked at him, clapping her hands together. "Do you not think we might be happy together. You with those muscles, and me the queen. We could be most wonderful together." She turned to face him, her face suddenly cold. "Do you not want to marry me?"

"I wouldnae risk provoking a war."

"You are the foolish idiot son of a blacksmith. I offer you a kingdom and you turn me down. I can't believe you would do that. I hate you."

She marched past him without another word, vanishing down the stairs and leaving him utterly bewildered.

None of it made any sense. Was she serious? Was she joking? Then as the forge was forbidden from being lit, he'd gone fishing. Lilias had brought him flowers and he got his second marriage proposal in one day.

He looked up at the windows of the great hall. Was Margaret telling them all about it? Or was she going to pretend nothing had happened?

His continued his search for Lilias but it proved fruitless. No doubt she was in the hall with Margaret. Eventually, he made his way to his chamber.

If it wasn't for Margaret's locket on his bed, he might have been able to convince himself he'd imagined the entire thing. But there it was, proof he hadn't made it up. She had come to him and proposed, no doubt part of an enormous joke.

"Are ye all right, son?"

He turned to find his father standing in the doorway. "You are no joining them for dinner?"

"I havenae any appetite."

"You're no wearing your mother's locket. It's tae keep ye safe, ye ken?"

"I took it off tae go swimming." The lie came quickly to his lips. He did not want to burden his father with the truth. He looked tired enough. He had been working night and day for weeks in preparation for the arrival of the princess, forging new swords to be given to her retinue as gifts from the clan.

"What happened?" Fingal asked, coming in and closing the door behind him. "Something ails ye."

Before he could answer there was a sound on the roof above them. A scraping and then a scream falling past the window. By the time Tavish looked out, it was too late. The princess was dead, her body laid below them in the courtyard.

He should have run. He should have left the castle with his father. The two of them had survived living off the land before. They could do it again. But how could he have known that within an hour he'd be hauled before the laird? That Lilias would point an accusing finger at him and tell the story that soon spread across the Highlands like wildfire. "You killed her, Tavish Sinclair. You pushed her from your window."

"Why?" someone shouted from the packed crowd, all of them eager to get a glimpse of the accused. Questions were thrown his way but his answers were lost in the noise.

"She spurned his advances," Lilias screamed, her face a picture of aggrieved innocence. She spat the words out, her face turning bright red. "He threw her to her death."

The crowd gasped.

Tavish looked around. Was there no one who believed him? "I didnae," he said but his voice was drowned by the noise.

His father waited until there was a lull to speak. "He was with me the entire time."

The laird called for silence as the noises of the crowd grew louder once more. "You believe in your son's innocence, Fingal Sinclair?"

Fingal nodded. "He has nothing to do with this."

"A princess lays dead in the chapel. A nation mourns. We are without an heir. You swear your son had no part to play?"

"I swear."

"Then how does he account for the fact that when her highness was reached in the courtyard, his mother's locket was found in her clenched fist?"

"She took it from me," Tavish said. "I swear it."

"A princess stealing from a blacksmith's son?" Lilias shouted. "She tore it from his neck as she fell," Lilias shouted at the top of her voice. "I saw it happen. Murderer!"

"Murderer!" The word began to echo around the room. Tavish looked from face to face, people he'd known since childhood. They were all twisted with rage, all except his father who was begging them to listen. None did.

He awoke in the dark to echo of their voices still screaming for his death. He might as well plead with the echo as with the clan. His fate was sealed.

Unless he could get this strange woman to help. He lay back down, an idea forming in his mind.

❦

Tavish awoke to find Lindsey nudging the fire back into life. "Morning," she said as he sat up and stretched. "How do you feel?"

He grunted in response. "Ye managed to relight the fire."

"I'm not totally useless," she said with a smile. "Look, I'm going home and I might never get the chance again to find out the truth. What happened, with the princess I mean?"

He told her what had happened, the dream all too fresh in his mind. When he was done, he finished by saying, "They locked my father in the dungeon and told me he would be killed if I ever returned to the castle. I was banished forever, told to be grateful for the mercy of the clan for not having me hung, drawn, and quartered."

He retrieved the last of the rabbit meat from the previous night and began to slice it into strips, struggling to cut through the burnt flesh with his blunt knife.

Lindsey was angry on his behalf, her chest puffing up as she spoke. "But Lilias lied. Why would she do that?"

He shrugged. "She was a child. She wanted revenge for me turning her down."

"But you could fix this. All you need to do is go see her and get her to confess. Don't you see? Get her to tell the truth about what happened and your father will be released. You'll be allowed back into the clan."

"I cannae go back without the stone or they'll kill ma father."

"What stone?"

About a week after they were accepted into the clan, Quinn came to fetch Tavish. "Come with me," the old druid said. "I have something to show you."

Together, they swam across the loch to the island. Tavish climbed out to find Quinn already at the well. How could someone so old swim so fast? He stood shivering as Quinn looked down into the depths of darkness. "Do you know what this is, Tavish?"

"A well."

Quinn smiled. "It is and it isn't. It is a portal."

"A portal?"

"There are many dotted across the Highlands. Places where the gap between times grows thin. Do you understand?"

"Not really."

"Do you know why you came to the castle?"

"We were hungry."

"No, it was more than that. You were meant to come. It was the first step toward something much bigger than you know. One day you'll understand. One day you'll meet someone who will retrieve the stone and save the clan. When they appear, you must do something for me Tavish. Can you swear you will do me one thing?"

"What is it?"

"It is vitally important she thinks it's her decision."

"Who? What are ye talking about?"

"Just promise me."

"Ah promise."

He wished he could remember what else Quinn had told him after that. He could only hope it came back to him when they made it to the island. Something important, something he'd long forgotten in the lonely years of exile.

"Clan Sinclair has a stone sacred to us all. The seat of the laird. The MacIntyres stole it a generation ago. At my trial they told me if I brought the stone back, I would prove my innocence."

"So why not go get the stone?"

"Because the MacIntyres would recognize me from a mile off and I'd be dead before I even caught a glimpse of it. MacIntyre Castle is the best defended in the Highlands. Surrounded by mountains and with only one way in or out. It would need a stranger to get in there and retrieve it."

"So. Don't you want to try?"

"They know what ah look like. I wouldnae stand a chance."

She stood up, an odd smile on her face as she

rubbed the back of her neck. "They know what you look like but they don't know what I look like."

He didn't let it show on his face but he was pleased. It had worked. Best of all, she'd thought it was her idea. He might be able to go back to the clan with a clean record at last, put all this behind him.

Chapter Five

"You cannae do this."

He was on his feet, standing perfectly still, looking more like an immovable boulder than a man. "You'll get yourself killed for nae good reason."

Lindsey tried to explain her plan again. "It's simple enough. I go into the castle, get this sacred stone of yours out. You take it home. Your father's let out of the dungeon and you get Lilias to confess she made the whole thing up out of jealousy. Then and only then, I go home."

"Why would ye take such a risk for me?"

She didn't speak for a moment. She wasn't sure how to word it. She couldn't exactly say it was because when she first suggested it he had smiled and the smile had lit up his face. Getting the stone would mean seeing that smile again and she wanted to see it again. Who went on a suicide mission to make a man smile? It was insane.

"It's because it's an injustice that I can help to right," she said at last. It's as much for my mom as for you. She believed you were innocent. This will help prove it. We might even be able to change the history books. You vanished after you were sent into exile. Did you know that? You were never seen again. This could change all that. The rest of your life might yet be written."

She also thought but didn't say out loud, and if you happen to hide Margaret's locket somewhere at your old house while I watch to see where it's hidden? Well, that would be quite a nice bonus.

"I cannae let you dae it. It's too dangerous. We should get ye back tae your time where ye belong."

"Let me do this for you. I want to help. Just think, a couple of days and you could be reunited with your father, your name cleared. What might the history books say about you then?"

He looked at her closely, his eyes fixed on hers. All of a sudden, she felt completely naked. Then he blinked and the feeling ended leaving her confused, her arms folding across her chest.

"All right," he said. "On your heed be it. If there's the slightest hint of danger though, we turn back. Agreed?"

"Agreed."

"Then I better hide the boat until we come this way again."

She watched as he dragged the boat back into the undergrowth, covering it with weeds until it was completely hidden from view. "Now we head north," he said.

"Will we get to see your house on the way?"

"Maybe. Why dae ye ask?"

"No reason. I'm just curious."

She thought about the ruin her mom had bought, how different it might look in its prime. Would it be weed covered like in her day, the start of its long decline?

Would she be able to persuade him to hide the locket somewhere inside on the way? What if he thought that was the only reason she was doing this? For the money the locket would raise?

They spent some time in the hut before setting off. Tavish packed a knapsack with dried rabbit meat and berries, filling a leather pouch with water from the loch before tying the end with twine.

While he picked supplies, Lindsey hung her modern clothes from a rusty hook in the ceiling. They should be dry by the time she got back, ready to head home again. How long until then?

She watched Tavish gather the last few things. "Ye are sure ye wish to dae this?" he asked as he picked up the knapsack. "Once we begin, there's nae turning back. The roads are too well guarded."

"I want to help you clear your name."

"Then let's get going before the light fades."

She had plenty of time to think while they traveled the long road north.

Whenever Tavish saw someone appear in the distance he grabbed Lindsey by the hand, pulling her into the bushes until the danger of being spotted had passed.

He never said what would happen if they were caught but she could guess. Death for the pair of them. The thought terrified her but still, she didn't suggest turning back. Nor did she tell him not to grab her hand.

Should she have gone home? Already she was starting to regret her decision. Each mile took her further away from the loch and every step north meant one more step back when they were done.

The place was dangerous, she could tell by the few villages they risked walking through. Suspicious eyes observed them both as they passed by despite their attempts to disguise their appearance.

Tavish had provided them with a hooded cloak each. Lindsey tried not to think about where they'd come from. She'd stood outside the tumbledown cottage with its thatched roof rotten and slumped to ground level in places.

When Tavish pushed open the door she caught a glimpse of a skeletal foot before turning away, trying not to retch from the smell. He came back out a moment later with two cloaks, passing one to her.

"What happened in there?" She asked.

He shrugged. "They're dead, looked like the work of the English tae me."

"Dead? Doesn't anyone care?"

"Since Margaret died the English dart north and kill any they find on their travels. We need the clans tae come together to stop the slaughter of innocents."

"They didn't get you though."

"I ken where to hide. Ah warned them two to

run but they wouldnae listen and now they've paid the price. Now put the cloak on, we want tae stay hidden."

He threw the hood over his head. Lindsey looked down at the heavy dark wool in her hand. There was a hint of the odor of decay drifting from it.

"I don't know if I can wear this."

He glared from under his cloak. "You wear it." His voice was dangerously low. "Now let's move."

They continued north with Lindsey wondering if she'd made a mistake in agreeing to this. He was scaring her but she had to admit the cloak was keeping her warm and protecting her modesty better than the length of tartan across her chest.

It had been stolen from the dead by someone who seemed indifferent to the two bodies he'd encountered, people he'd once known by the sound of it.

She tried to shut her mind, pulling the hood further over her head. She'd made a decision, there was no point doing that if she was going to back out as soon as the first problem came along.

She wore her sneakers, but they were coated in mud within half a mile of setting off and soon looked no different to Tavish's boots.

Her feet began to ache as she traveled north, the blisters on her feet growing so sore she found herself limping the further the day wore on. She could have been home safe and sound, soaking her feet in hot water.

She almost laughed. What hot water? The electric had been cut off at the house.

What was she going back to anyway? Without knowing where the locket was hidden, there didn't seem much point in going back to her own time.

She found herself watching Tavish as he marched ahead of her. He was like a machine, never tiring, never pausing for breath. He just kept going. He didn't even stumble when they passed through a swampy morass of mud, Lindsey falling far behind. The guy was inhuman.

At last, she had no choice. "Wait," she said, so far back he was almost out of sight. In the distance "I need to rest."

He looked back, his eyebrows raising. "Does no one march in your time?"

"Not like this," she replied as he headed back to where she'd stopped. "When people walk in my time, they do it for fun."

"For fun?"

"For pleasure. For recreation, you know?"

"People walk for enjoyment?" He ran his hand through his hair while shaking his head. "Not to get somewhere?"

"Well, sometimes. But we have cars and buses too if we want to get somewhere far." She saw the confused look on his face. "Like carriages but faster."

"With more horses, you mean?"

"Something like that. We can get going again if you like. Just please go a little slower."

"Another hour and we'll stop for the night. There's a hamlet not far from here. We may be able to scavenge some food there too."

"Scavenge? Why scavenge, why not buy?"

"I have little coin. Do you?"

"No, but-"

"Then we find what's thrown away or we go hungry. Your choice."

He started walking again. Had she offended him? It was hard to tell. Apart from that flicker of a smile on the beach, he looked furious all the time, as if he was angry with the whole world.

She couldn't blame him, not really. She'd be pretty cross if she'd been accused of a murder she didn't commit. She tried to think how she'd feel if her mom was locked in prison for trying to defend her.

The emotion made her neck hurt from tensing her jaw so much. She realized her fists had clenched and had to force them to loosen. If he wanted to look cross, she understood where he was coming from.

Not for much longer though. They would get to MacIntyre Castle, as long as her feet survived the journey. Then she would get the stone. He could go back to his life and she could go back to hers. Tell mom where he hid the locket, sell it, make a fortune, and finally do up the house.

She dreamed of carving the banisters, using her whittling skills to create little statues and Celtic symbols, make the place seem like home.

"Haud up," Tavish said, raising his arm, fist clenched.

Lindsey froze, expecting to dive into the bushes yet again.

"Wait there," Tavish said, darting off the road and into a copse of trees. She looked but saw nothing. Then a twig snapped and a moment later a straggly looking horse burst out into the open.

It galloped straight at her but saw her at the last minute, pulling up short and stopping dead.

"Whoah," Tavish said behind it, moving slowly toward it, arms outstretched. "Whoah there, lass."

He moved until he was in front of the horse and then began whispering something to it, talking so quietly Lindsey couldn't make out more than a word or two. He was speaking a language she didn't understand but the horse did.

The beast stamped its feet and whinnied loudly but then its ears went up as it listened. Another stamp of its foot but this one less aggressive and accompanied by a slight flick of its tail.

He continued talking to it and, as he did so, it lowered its head, allowing him to scratch it behind the ears. "That's it, lass," he said quietly. "Good girl." He glanced across at Lindsey. "You can climb on."

"You're not serious?"

"She willnae hurt you. Not now."

Lindsey wasn't so confident. She took a step forward and the horse's head jerked in her direction, its nostrils flaring. Another few words from Tavish and it calmed once more, this time looking at her placidly.

"I can't believe I'm doing this," she said as she climbed onto a tree stump. "No saddle or anything.

You know I've only ridden a horse once, don't you?"

"Wild horses like wild women."

"Are you saying I'm a wild woman?"

He looked up at her, his expression inscrutable. "Was that a joke?" she asked. "Did you actually make a joke?"

There it was, that flicker of a smile again. She couldn't help reciprocating. "I didn't think you were capable of joking."

This close, the horse smelt strongly, Lindsey's nose wrinkling as she climbed onto its back.

It didn't move a muscle. She tensed her legs, expecting the animal to throw her at any moment.

It felt utterly surreal when, a second later, Tavish began walking again. The horse followed meekly behind like a pet dog, carrying Lindsey on its back without the slightest complaint.

Once she had gotten over her fear of being thrown, she began to enjoy the ride. Her aching feet were glad of the break from walking. "Thank you," she said when Tavish stopped to let the horse drink from a stream beside the road.

"What for? Helping you doon?"

"For this. For letting me ride her."

He shrugged. "It wasnae any bother."

"Thank you anyway."

They set off again a minute later, stopping when they reached a tiny little settlement nestled in a hidden valley. There were two little cottages to the left of the road separated by a pond. On the right was a broch that had been altered over time, wooden planks added where the stone had crumbled.

All the buildings were topped by thatch and smoke was curling up through them into the evening sky, the smell reminding Lindsey of the campfires she'd experienced back when her mom was well enough to take her out into the wilderness.

That was where she first learned about wood carving, those trips together. She examined the carved S in the doorframe of the nearest farm-house, a crude face had been scored below, marked deep into the wood.

The face had been painted a long time ago, the colors faded to little more than grays and browns, hard to see in the dying light. How would some-thing like that look on Tavish's house when she got back?

"We may find shelter here for the night," Tavish said, bringing the horse to a stop. He held out a hand to Lindsey and she took it, her tiny fingers swallowed by his massive fist as he effortlessly lifted her from the horse, his hands sliding to grab her waist when she began to fall.

He set her down on the ground. The feel of his hands on her remained for some time after he stepped back. She shook the feeling away, watching as he slapped the horse on the rear a moment later. "Off you go, lass."

Lindsey knew she was imagining it but the neigh the horse gave sounded very much like it under-stood what Tavish had said. It vanished back the way it came, leaving the two of them alone.

The sun finally vanished behind the rolling hills in the distance, the land turning shades of red, making it look like the fields were on fire.

They walked toward the nearest building. From inside they could hear a woman singing. "The Highland lassie waits long for her man. He will nay come this way ever again."

"I ken that wee ditty," Tavish said, putting his ear to the door. "My father used to sing it to me when I was a bairn."

He knocked on the door while Lindsey attempted to imagine him as a child. She couldn't do it no matter how hard she tried.

The singing stopped and the door scraped open,

revealing a woman in her thirties, hair as red as the setting sun. "What do ye want?" she asked, her eyes narrowing.

Tavish kept his head hidden under his hood as he spoke. "We are pilgrims from the south o' your land. We seek shelter for the night."

"You'll get none here."

"Who is it, Agnes?" a voice shouted from inside.

"Beggars," she yelled back. "You keep stirring the broth. Merida'll be hungry as a bear when she wakes."

"We will sleep in yon barn," Tavish said. "It wasnae a request."

The man appeared, a red-headed infant in his arms. "Ye can sleep in the stable if ye be Christians. Heathen English plague these lands and the cattle stopped milking last time they were here."

"Ah am indebted tae ye," Tavish said, clasping his hands together before the woman could contradict her husband.

"It's behind the house," the woman said. "Mind ye dinnae touch anything in there. I ken how many turnips are nestled in the straw."

She closed the door a second later. Before they'd taken two steps it opened again and out was thrust a pair of apples without a word. Tavish took them and nodded his thanks to the already closed door.

"This way," he said, passing her an apple as he walked around the woodpile to the back of the house. A barn was sticking out of the rear of the building, the sweet smell of straw emanating from inside.

Two minutes later Lindsey was nestled comfortably in the straw, her eyes sagging almost at once. Her thighs ached from gripping the horse and she was desperate to soak her aching feet.

She settled for removing her sneakers and socks, lying back on the straw and munching the apple as Tavish looked out the barn door to the countryside beyond.

Her eyes closed before she knew what was happening. The next thing she knew she was dreaming. She knew it was a dream because she was back home. Mom was asleep in the chair by the tiny little single bar electric heater. It glowed orange but she couldn't feel the heat from it. That was strange. At least Mom had persuaded them to turn the electricity back on.

"Where are you?" Rhona asked in her sleep.

"I'm coming back," Lindsey replied. Her mom

stirred but didn't open her eyes. "I'll be home soon, mom."

"Are you safe?" Rhona asked, still not opening her eyes.

"I'm safe. I'm with Tavish Sinclair."

"Hmm." A smile played across Rhona's face as she twisted in the chair, her legs stretching out toward the fire. "Be careful."

"He's a good man, mom. You were right. He didn't kill Margaret."

The dream began to fade. A mist started to fill the room, coming between her and her mother. "The locket's coming, Mom. It's all going to be all right. I promise." She shouted the last words but by then the dream had faded and she was sitting up in the barn, not sure what was real and what wasn't.

She turned for comfort from Tavish but he wasn't there. She looked around in a panic. Had he left her alone? She had no clue how to get back to the loch on her own. "Tavish?" she called out. "Where are you?"

The door to the barn swung open and he appeared. "What's wrong? Are ye all right?"

"Oh, Tavish. I thought you'd gone. I was so scared."

"I went tae fetch some breakfast. Here, carrots."

"Oh," she said, already feeling embarrassed by how worried she'd been. "Thank you."

It was some time before her heart had slowed sufficiently for her to feel hungry. As she nibbled on the end of the carrot, Tavish went again without a word, this time coming back with a jug of water and a horn mug. "Drink," he said. "We've a long walk ahead of us today."

"Great," she said, rubbing her feet. "More walking."

He frowned as he glanced down. "You're bleeding. Why did ye nae say so?"

"It's nothing. I'm just not used to so much walking."

"Wait there."

For the third time, he vanished. This time he was gone for a while. Lindsey drank a mugful of water and finished the carrot, finding a hidden spot far away from the barn to use the bathroom while he was gone. When he finally came back, he found her washing her face with the last of the water.

"Sit doon," he said, pointing to the straw.

"What's that in your hand?"

"You'll see. Take them stockings off."

"They're called socks."

"Whatever they are, get them off."

She did as he asked. He took some of the leaves he'd gathered and dipped them in the remains of the water. Mashing them into a ball he added the rest until the water was no more than a pile of green mush.

"Lift your leg ontae my lap," he said, sitting opposite her.

He took hold of her ankle, working the mash into the worst of her blisters. Almost at once the pain began to subside. Lindsey sighed, the relief palpable as he continued to work the rest of the poultice into her foot. "Now put your sock over it," he said, swapping to her other foot after she'd done as he asked.

"What is that?" she asked.

"Is it helping?"

"It's wonderful."

"A few decent leaves can ease the ache o' many things," he replied. "How do ye feel?"

"Much better, thank you." She pulled her sock up as he got to his feet.

She sat still for a moment, watching as he carried the water outside. An odd question entered her mind from nowhere. What if I stay?

She shook her head. That wasn't something she should waste any time contemplating. Yes, he was handsome. She'd got her first close look at him while he'd eased the pain in her feet. Those dark eyes that smoldered whenever he glanced up at her, that jaw that looked as if it could take an ax blow with no damage other than the weapon snapping in half.

Yes, behind his gruff exterior there lay hid a gentleman. The touch of his hands on her feet would have told her that if she hadn't already worked it out.

None of it mattered though. What mattered was that her mom still needed her. It might have been a dream but the sight of her mom sitting alone by the fire tugged at her heart. She needed to focus on hiding the locket somewhere they could find it in the future. Help him get the stone back and he'd be grateful enough to do that in return, she was sure of it.

She had to focus, not get distracted by how good he looked framed in the doorway by the morning sun. She got to her feet, hoping to leave all those thoughts behind her in the barn. "Shall we get going?"

"Aye, lass. And look who came back."

The horse appeared next to him, nudging its nose under his arm, sniffing out the carrot in his hand. "All right, lass," he said with a smile. "I see you're no tired of our company yet. Or is it just ye want some breakfast as well."

It took seconds for the horse to demolish the carrot and then it stood ready and waiting. Tavish held out a hand. "Shall ah lift ye onto her back?"

"You should ride. I'll walk. I rode yesterday."

"Your feet are hurting. Ahm used to marching."

"They're not hurting now. I don't mind walking. You should ride. You tamed the thing."

"Ahm no arguing. You ride."

"This is stupid."

"Aye, it is. If it'll stop your blether we'll both ride."

He lifted her onto the horse before she could complain, his hands again around her waist to hoist her up. She almost fell but he noticed before she did, his hand in the small of her back, pushing her back into place.

With no apparent effort, he leaped straight up behind her, shuffling close to scratch the horse between its ears. "You do well to carry us both, lass," he said as the horse began to move. "Stronger than you look."

Lindsey had the strangest feeling he was talking to her rather than the horse. She shook the feeling away as his hands slid back until they were holding her waist. She tried to ignore the tensing up of her body as they rode slowly away from the barn.

"On the back of this lass we should be there in a few days," Tavish said.

The sooner the better, Lindsey thought. And the sooner his hands were off her the better.

Chapter Six

꧁꧂

Tavish had not been this close to another person in years. Did she know she had reached out for his hand in her sleep? That she'd twisted and turned and grumbled, only settling when he put a hand on her forehead, shushing her gently, telling her it would be okay.

He'd sung the songs of the Highlands under his breath, watching in the darkness of the barn until she settled once more, the discomfort fading from her face.

He'd looked at her for some time before laying back down in the straw. She looked pretty in her sleep, her fiery red hair falling around her face, that tension was gone from her jaw and neck.

While he'd waited for sleep to come, he'd

wondered why she was doing this. There must be more to it than fulfilling Quinn's wish. She didn't know him, she had no reason to help him and yet she was. He found himself drawn to her yet he knew there was no point to the feeling.

Once they retrieved the stone, she'd go back to her own time where she belonged. She wasn't even born yet. It was a strange feeling to ride behind a ghost. That was what she was, not a person of his time, a spirit passing through.

"Tell me about yourself," she said as they passed through a thick wood of oak, the branches reaching together over their head to block out the sun.

"There's nothing tae tell."

"Come on. You must have a past. Everyone does."

"What do you want to ken?"

"I want to know if the history books have got anything right about you."

"What dae they say about me?" He was intrigued despite himself. It was strange to think that he would feature in any books. "Do they talk only of the death o' the princess?"

"Not at all. The one I was reading had quite a lot about you."

"Like what?"

"That you were born into the poorest village in the clan, that you and your father left when the plague struck, that you were close to becoming laird in waiting when…"

He waited but she didn't continue so he took over. "When Margaret died and they threw me oot. I ken that part. What did it say about me after that?"

"Nothing. You vanished. There were a couple of theories. One said you'd been executed in secret. Another said you'd joined the English army. My mom said once she thought you'd become a monk."

Silence fell once more. Tavish found himself wanting to keep the conversation going. It was an odd feeling. "Tell me about you," he asked.

"My life's nowhere near as interesting as yours."

There was a coldness to her voice that intrigued him. Why shut down the conversation so quickly when it turned to her? "You have a life at home, don't you?"

"Not much of one. I work in a cafe, I live with my mom. I've not exactly got a lot going for me."

"What's a cafe?"

"Like a tavern."

"You're a kitchen wench?"

"I'm not sure I'd use that term but yeah, sure."

"You sound like you dinnae care for the work."

"I don't."

"Why not?"

"Because my boss is a dick. Can we talk about something else?"

"Any men in your life?"

She glanced behind her and he pointedly looked back without blinking. Let her think what she wanted. She looked coldly into his face before turning away.

She clearly wasn't interested in him and that irritated him for a reason he couldn't really explain. He should have been glad. Scratch that, he was glad.

"No," she said at last, looking back again. "No men in my life. What about you?"

"No men in my life either."

She laughed out of nowhere and the sound lightened him. "That was another joke," she said. "You're full of surprises, aren't you?"

"If you've no men tae go back to and you dinnae like your job, why do you care about going back?"

"Because of my mom."

"Are you no old enough to survive without her?"

"Says the man who wants to do this to get his father out of a dungeon."

"That's different."

"Why?"

"Is your mother chained up in the dark being fed nothing but bread and water?"

She shook her head, glancing back at him again, her lips pursed. "I'm sorry," she said. "I didn't mean to be rude."

"It disnae matter."

"I need to get back to look after her. She bought your old house and she's been doing it up as a kind of memorial to you, but we ran out of money."

She fell silent, her shoulders visibly sagging.

"What?" Tavish asked. "What ails ye?"

"Where are you going to hide the locket. If I can tell mom where it is when we get back, we can sell it and make enough to do the house back up. I wasn't going to say anything but darn it, you just have a way of getting these things out of me."

"I havenae hidden the locket. I carry it still."

"But you have to hide it. All the history books say you hid it. It's somewhere in the house but no one knows where."

"Why do you want to fix my house anyway?"

"I don't but mom does. I want to help her. You must understand that."

He glanced further down the road, noticing too late that a group of men on horseback was approaching. He cursed himself for getting distracted by their conversation. "Haud on," he said, reaching past her to tap the horse on the side of its neck.

With a kick to its flanks at the same time, it understood what was needed, turning at once and darting into the trees.

"Keep quiet," he whispered, pushing branches out of the way as they rode deeper. He should have been paying attention to the road, not to her. If they were to have any chance of surviving this, he needed to concentrate better.

When they were unable to move any deeper into the trees he stopped, climbing down from the horse and edging back toward the road, listening hard.

There had been three of them, all dressed in the tartan of the Sinclairs. He could only hope they thought he was a bandit and not worth chasing. He only had his sword and it had been a long time since he'd used it in anger.

Slipping from one tree trunk to another he

reached the road and took a deep breath before peering out. There was no one there. He was about to step back when he felt the tip of a sword blade at the base of his neck.

"Dinnae move," a voice said.

The man was good. No one could sneak up on him unless he'd trained them himself.

His instincts kicked in at once. Leaning back, he feinted right then dropped down an instant later, the sword left hanging in empty air. On his back, he lashed out with his feet, bringing his attacker down to the ground with a grunt.

The other two were running at him from behind a tree to his left. He braced himself for their arrival, springing back to his feet, sword in hand. His hood fell back from his face.

"Come on then," he snapped. "I'll have your heeds on a platter." At once his assailants stopped dead.

"Tavish?" one said. "Is that ye?"

He squinted, examining the two men closely as the third got slowly to his feet.

"Tavish," the fallen man said, slapping his arm. "Good tae see you again."

"Who are you?" he asked.

"Do you nae recognize us now we're grown and wi' beard?"

The voice rang a bell. He scrutinised them further before speaking. "Billy? Jock? And is that wee Matthew?"

"Aye. Wit are ye deein' so close to Castle MacIntyre? Have you got the stone? If any could get it, ah've no doubt it'd be you."

"Nae but ah'm on me way tae fetch it. Have ye news of me father?"

"Aye. He lives still. Quinn tends to him daily. The druid's the only one the laird dare not cross."

Tavish's breath caught in his throat. He coughed to clear it. "Good." With the druid looking after his father, he could be sure of his safety.

"We'll tell him you're alive. He'll be awfa glad."

"Tell him ah will see him again soon."

There was a noise from the road, a horse riding by at speed. Matthew peered out from the trees. "We must go. We cannae be seen talking to ye."

"You're old enough to patrol? Ah remember when none of ye would leave the castle for fear o' the English."

"Aye, well," Jock said, blushing behind his beard. "That were long ago."

Billy smiled. "And we have you to thank for

keeping us alive this long. You were the best sword-master a boy could wish for. Trained us to be silent as the crypt. Did ye really no hear us creeping up on ye?"

"Ye have learned well, the three of ye."

"Always with the same start to every bout," Matthew said. "Come on then."

They all said at once, "I'll have your heeds on a platter."

The group laughed and Tavish found himself laughing with them. It was a strange sound, his chest rumbling with it.

Billy was the first to turn serious. "It's because of your training that we survived going to war. They were fools to send you away. It was an awfa shame wit they deed to ye. We tried to make the laird see reason, but he wouldnae listen."

"Let's no talk of that," Tavish said. "Ahm glad ye are all well. Get gone. Ah've no wish tae cause ye bother."

"Listen, Tavish. Be careful. The MacIntyres would be awfa glad of an excuse to besiege the Sinclairs. Ah hope ye have a good plan for getting the stone."

Tavish nodded. "Ah do."

The three of them were gone without another

sound. It was as if they'd never been there. They had learned well.

"Who was that?"

He almost jumped. He'd been so lost in thought he hadn't noticed the horse making its way back to him, Lindsey still sitting on its back.

"Ah thought I told you to stay hidden."

"I tried but this horse of yours has a mind of her own. She was coming back to you with or without me. Who were they? Are we in danger?"

"From Billy, Jock, and Matthew? They were the three smallest bairns I ever taught war tae."

"They didn't look that small to me."

"A decade older than when ah last saw them. I remember them crashing through the woods when ah was trying tae teach them tae track silently."

"Looks like it finally paid off."

"What makes ye say that?"

"I saw them sneaking up on you. They were like ghosts. I didn't even hear the leaves rustle under their feet."

"You saw them and they didnae see you? You've got hidden talents, lass. Come on, we better get moving. We have a way to go yet."

He climbed up behind her and brought the horse back onto the road. Glancing both ways before setting off he vowed not to lose concentration again. He spoke little until they stopped for the night.

"Where are we?" she asked as he headed off the road, following a stream downhill into a glen. "Do you know where we're going?"

"Aye, this is the land o' my childhood. The village I grew up in is over the next hill and glen."

"Does that mean your old house is near here somewhere?"

"Aye. About a mile that way."

"Can we see it? I mean if we keep going, please."

"We will be spending the night there."

He took the familiar trail, the one he'd never forgotten. The path was overgrown, little wonder since the house had been empty so long. Through the glen and out the other side and then along a cut between two hills, a winding valley that came out in a wide opening.

There at the far end was the looming bulk of Garra Fell.

They rode on as the last of the light died. It didn't matter anymore. He could have traveled this stretch blindfolded, the memory of this land had never faded, not in all the years he'd been away.

As they rode, his hand went to the pocket in his hose. He felt for the locket and a thought occurred to him.

She looked back at him, her eyes glittering in the moonlight, looking like tiny stars.

He liked it when she looked at him. There was no denying she was a pretty enough lass, even if her face spent most of its time hidden under the hood of her cloak.

He noticed his breathing had loosened as if the air grew thinner. It was just the fell.

So why was his heart pounding? It was because he was nearly home, that was all.

They crested the fell and there it was, he was home. She turned and looked where he was pointing. "Ma hoose."

He had no idea what he expected her to say but the last thing he expected was for her to burst into tears.

"What's wrong?" he asked, putting an arm around her shoulder, drawing her back toward him. "What's the matter?"

"Nothing," she said quietly. "I'm fine."

Chapter Seven

Lindsey felt far from fine even as she forced the words out. She swallowed her sadness, trying to make the tears stop.

Tavish climbed down from the horse first, leaving it to munch the grass beside the entrance to the house.

That was where mom's car was. The horse was standing on the exact spot where their clapped out old red Ford sat waiting to die.

"What's the matter?" he asked again, reaching up with his hand to help her down.

As she climbed down, she almost stumbled, her vision blurred. He took hold of her and didn't let go, his arms around her waist. He drew her to him, and her head fell into the crook of his shoulder.

The tears grew heavier. He said nothing, just held her there. She could feel the warmth of his chest through his cloak, the slow and steady breathing that did not change the entire time he was holding her.

If only it could work, she thought, and that sent a fresh batch of tears to her eyes. She stamped her feet, determined to stop it. What good would crying do? It wouldn't get her back to her mom. She'd made her decision. She had to help him first.

She was no longer sure why she was crying. Was it because she was again wondering what it would be like to stay with him? Or was it because seeing the house had brought it all back.

"I miss my mom," she said quietly, her voice muffled by his chest.

He still didn't say anything, his arms gripping her tightly, giving her time. It was time she badly needed.

She felt exhausted all of a sudden, her legs turning weak. When he took her hand to lead her inside, she didn't complain.

The house had clearly been empty for some time but it was still in much better shape than in her time.

He brushed debris aside from a chair, and then

eased her into it, dragging over another chair before once again taking her hand.

"It'll be all right." He looked like he was about to say something but then he didn't. "There is nothing wrong wi' missing her," he said at last.

"It's not just that," she replied, pulling her hand away to wipe her face, sniffing loudly as she did so. "Attractive, yeah?"

He shrugged but said nothing.

"It's just seeing the house, it reminded me of everything. She's taken care of me ever since dad ran out on us both. I don't know how she did it, juggling work and baby me. Then she got sick and now she's better but I can't help her. Somehow, she managed and we survived. I've spent all my life wanting to make it up to her and I can't and it kills me."

She looked up at him as he cleared his throat. "Ma father told me something when ah was wee."

"What?"

"He said no parent looks after their children for reward. They do it because it's the right thing to do, you ken? Your mother didnae look after you so you could pay her back later. She did it because she loved you."

Lindsey's shoulders hitched but she managed to

keep the tears at bay. "I know she loves me. When she was ill, I had to drop out of school and get work or we'd have been homeless. I never got the qualifications for a decent job.

"I've spent my whole life wanting to help her and instead I feel like I've been treading water the whole time. If I stop, we both might drown and here I am gallivanting around while she's at home with no money and no hope of getting this place fixed."

"You dinnae know what the future might bring."

"Easy for you to say. I could just bring you the book of your life and you'd know everything about the future."

He shook his head. "Your book can say what it wants. Ah ken it has no been written yet. Ma future isn't set until ah make it. You already said ah vanish. What if ye coming back here has changed all that?"

She frowned then shook her thoughts away. "Are you going to give me the tour or what?"

It was surreal to walk through the house with him. By modern standards the place wasn't large but compared to the villages they'd traveled through it was a decent enough size, spread across two floors.

The first floor consisted of an entrance hallway with a kitchen to the left, the fireplace in the middle of the room.

"No chimney," Lindsey noted, remembering what she'd learned about this era, that in most places the smoke rose from a central fireplace up through the thatch, choking the lice and fleas on the way.

There was a roof above the kitchen, the only one-story part of the building. The other side of the hallway was the room they'd first entered.

"This was the main living area," Tavish said. "I remember ma father sitting me on his knee by that window, looking out at the village green. The trees were always full of apples in ma memory. This way."

He led her back into the hallway and she stopped at the foot of the stairs. "What?" he asked, watching her run her hand up the newel post.

"The carving," she said. "It's beautiful."

He looked at the intricate Celtic swirls, the paint long faded. "My grandfather made it."

"He was a talented man." She smiled to herself. That would be the perfect tribute to Tavish. She would recreate that design when they rebuilt the staircase.

BLANCHE DABNEY

She followed him up the stairs, admiring each baluster as she went. "It was the Sinclair symbol," Tavish said, seeing where she was looking.

"An S that repeats," she replied. "I see it."

He raised his eyebrows before turning away and vanishing through another door. "There's not much upstairs in my time," she said when she caught up with him.

"This was my room," he said. "It's a rare thing to have your own room, you ken? Ma grandfather kept the bairns in here while he was next door with his missus."

"It's nice seeing it with a roof on."

The plaster had crumbled in both rooms, but they still maintained a hint of their former warmth. It didn't take long for Tavish to clear the fireplace of debris.

"Chimney here," she said.

"We were the first tae have one. Only the castles have them around here."

"And the monasteries," Lindsey replied. "Or is that in a couple of years?"

"Ah dinnae ken," he said. "What matters is that this will keep ye warm tonight. Ah'll get the logs if you get the kindling."

They went back downstairs together and

headed outside. Lindsey began looking for dry twigs, not an easy task in the dark. She found herself continually glancing back at the house, comparing it to how it looked in her time.

It was a strange sight, seeing it still with all four walls and the thatched roof. The straw had slipped in places, but it would be a fair while before it fell away to expose the interior.

When she had two armfuls of kindling, she returned to the smaller of the two bedrooms, surprised to see Tavish already there.

"You move quietly," she said, dumping the kindling at his feet. "I didn't hear you come back."

"I've stuffed the bed with fresh straw and found a couple of blankets for ye." He turned away and began piling up kindling in the fireplace. His expression when he'd told her about the blankets made it look as if he was daring her to thank him.

She didn't, not wanting to embarrass him but silently she was grateful he'd gone to so much effort.

In no time at all the chill was gone from the room. Lindsey nestled in the straw, her cloak wrapped around her.

"I must find some way of washing tomorrow," she said to herself, the low light of the fire doing little to hide the buildup of grime on her skin.

"There's a loch near here," Tavish said.

"Did I say that out loud?"

"Aye lass, though you look clean enough to me."

"That's because it's dark in here."

"Ah see well enough. Are ye hungry?"

"Famished."

"I brought carrots from this morning and I set some traps while we were getting the fire going. Keep an eye on the fire."

"I'm not going anywhere." She lay back in the straw, her eyes closing. Her head ached from crying and she found herself wondering what her mom was up to at that moment. She was just downstairs, only a few feet away. And yet she might as well have been on another planet.

She had no idea how long Tavish was gone, but she must have fallen asleep as she stirred to the sight of him nudging the fire back into life.

"Sorry," she said before her eyes were even open. "I must have nodded off."

"It's nay bother," he replied, sitting on the edge of the bed, his hands pointed toward the fire. "Two rabbits soon cooked."

Lindsey was surprised by how loudly her stomach started growling as the smell of cooking filled the room.

"You miss your mother," Tavish said out of nowhere. "Don't you?"

"I do," she replied. "I hope she's all right."

He grabbed the rabbits from the spit and passed one to her. "Let it cool," he said, tearing a chunk from his own, steam billowing from his mouth.

"Have you got a cast iron stomach?" she asked. "How is that not burning you?"

He shrugged. "Ye can get used to anything given enough time."

"I don't think I'll ever get used to how dark it is here."

"It's no dark. We've got the light from the fire."

"I mean outside. I can't see a thing out there. In my time, there's always the glow of a town somewhere nearby but here, nothing. It's quiet too. I'm not used to that either."

His dark eyes fixed on her. "Do the books say anything about my mother?"

She shook her head. "Very little. What was she like?"

"She died giving birth to me. Ah never knew her. All ma father told me was she loved bluebells because they flowered all the way into summer up here. That's the carving above your bed there. A circle o' bluebells."

Lindsey glanced up at the ceiling. It looked as if just talking about it pained him and she was glad for an excuse to look away and let him compose himself.

She found herself dying to hug him like he'd done to her outside, comfort him, tell him it would be all right.

"You don't have to tell me if you don't want to."

"I never have told anyone. I dinnae ken. Mebbe it's because you're not from here but ah dinnae mind talking to ye. My father took good care of me and ah've let him down. This is ma chance to make it right.

"It was because of him that ah became a sword master, a teacher of war to the wee bairns at Castle Sinclair. He sacrificed everything to get me up the ladder toward laird and how did ah repay him?" He almost spat the words out. "I took to banishment like a fish to water. Ah should have fought them all."

"You couldn't fight an entire clan, not when everyone was against you."

"Billy, Jock, and Matthew weren't against me. For all I knew, there might have been more. He's in the dungeon and ah might no see him again if this doesnae work."

"It will work, you'll see."

He picked up a carrot and tore the end off, chewing it slowly.

Lindsey ate the rest of her rabbit in silence, laying down the bones next to the bed, a huge yawn spreading across her face, the natural result of being so close to such a warm fire. She sagged down onto her back on the bed.

"It'll be all right," she said. "I came back here for a reason. I know it's to help you."

"And your mother," Tavish replied. "Ah put Margaret's locket under the fireplace downstairs. It shouldnae be hard to find."

"You didn't have to," Lindsey said, craning her neck to look at him. He'd crossed to the doorway and was looking back at her.

"Ah ken what it's like to lose a parent," he said before disappearing into the darkness.

Lindsey lay back on the straw, listening to it rustle under her. She didn't hear a thing from the other room all night.

The fire snapped and crackled as the logs began to burn down. As her eyes closed, she thought about what he'd said and done for her. She could go home now. She knew where the locket was.

It would all be fine. They could sell it and do up

the house. She'd finally be able to see her mom living in comfort for the first time ever.

Not yet, she told herself. First, she had a promise to keep. She was going to get the sacred stone for him, see him reunited with his father. She might never have known hers, but she knew well enough the desire to help a parent.

That was the main thing they had in common. They'd both lost one parent and wanted to do what was right for the other. He had helped her, it was time to do the same.

She wondered if she could do something to say thank you for hiding the locket. An idea came to her and she fell asleep with a smile playing across her lips.

Chapter Eight

The next morning Tavish awoke early. He'd never found it easy to settle but being back in his old house had made it even harder.

He lay back on what used to be his parents' bed, half expecting them to come in and throw him out, ask him why he wasn't in his own bedroom.

He had lain back in the darkness, listening to the quiet breathing of Lindsey as she slept. She had that bad dream again, whatever it was that had disturbed her before.

He'd tiptoed through when she started moaning, shushing her quietly and holding her in his arms until she settled again. He refused to look at her as he comforted her.

If he looked at her, he knew what would happen. That weird feeling would bubble up again, the one he was determined to ignore.

Once he was sure she was calm he returned to his own bed and finally fell asleep, dreaming he was back home. He should have known at once it was a dream. His father was there. The house was crumbling due to a mist running through it.

The mist made holes appear wherever it struck, gaps in the ceiling that let in the daylight, holes in the floor. He was in his room playing with a wooden sword when he heard voices. He headed across the hall and found his parents talking. Neither of them noticed he was there.

"You have tae tell him," his mother was saying.

"I cannae," his father replied.

He lost the words as he stared at his mother. He'd never seen her, only heard her described by his father. Yet, he knew it was her. There was no doubt about it. She was beautiful, tall, hair tied in a coif, dress made of warm wool, tartan sash across her chest, locket around her neck.

She turned, noticing him standing there. "Hello, bonny boy," she said, kneeling down in front of him. "Haven't you grown so big since I last saw you?"

"Mother," he replied, his voice trembling. "Is that really you?" Mist rolled between them, her face becoming harder to see.

Her smile faded as the mist began to swallow her, a tear rolling down her cheek. "I dinnae have long. The stone will save the clan. You must return it. Quinn was right. She is the key. Protect her."

"I will, mother. I'm on my way. Are you really here?"

"I'm not as far away as you think. Tell your father I lo…"

The mist swallowed her up and then he was sitting up in bed, his heart pounding. He glanced around him. There was mist, rolling in through the shutterless window.

It was only a dream. She hadn't been there. He had imagined the whole thing.

He was on his feet a moment later. It might have been a dream, but he couldn't shake the idea that retrieving the stone was the key to everything.

The MacIntyres had stolen it a generation ago, besieging Castle Sinclair for months, grinding down the occupants. In the dead of night, a dozen of them had sneaked in and taken the stone.

The morale of the defenders had crumbled and the Sinclair Clan had paid dearly for that loss over the years, losing land and people to wars they should have easily defended.

With the English pushing at the borders and the Bruce still warring over Balliol's accession to the throne, the Sinclairs needed a symbol, something to bring them together and make them strong.

The stone would do it. He would bring it back to them. Getting Lilias to tell the truth wasn't important. Clearing his name wasn't important. What motivated him to get moving was finally having someone who could help get the stone back where it belonged.

He went through to wake Lindsey up. Her room was empty.

Where was she?

He ran over to the window and looked out. She'd run off, of course, no doubt to tell the MacIntyres he was coming. Could he catch her in time?

He sprinted down the stairs and outside in time to see her walking across the grass, something in her arms. Were they fish?

"I found the loch," she said, smiling as she approached him.

"Ah see you caught some fish."

"I borrowed your knife, I hope you don't mind."

He felt for his hip. The knife wasn't there. "When did you take that?"

"This morning. I was going to ask but you were fast asleep."

"You came into my room and stole my knife without waking me?"

"Are you angry?"

He couldn't help smiling. "No one has ever managed to do that, not in all the training I did with the clan. You must be quieter than the morning mist."

"Here," she said, passing him the knife and almost dropping the fish as she did so. "I used it for the hook and for…well, let's get some breakfast going shall we?"

"I'll get some more kindling."

"Already done, did it before I went fishing."

"How did you have time? When did you wake up?"

"Just before dawn. I know this is going to sound crazy, but I woke up hearing a woman talking in your room. I came to look but there was just you, fast asleep.

"I thought seeing as I was up, I might as well go look for that loch you were talking about. It's really beautiful over there, I can see why you lived here."

"I didnae have a choice. Did you see the village? Is it rebuilt?"

Her shoulders sagged slightly and she looked down at the ground before looking back up at him. "Empty and burned I'm afraid."

"When word o' the plague gets out, some think fire's the only cure. Is it ever rebuilt in the future?"

She shook her head. "There's no village there in my time. Just this house and then the forest below."

"What's done is done. Let's get the fire going. We have a long journey ahead of us today. Take ma flint while ah feed the horse."

She headed inside while he led the horse over to a lush patch of grass. He left it to eat, heading back to the house. He was almost inside when he decided to go see the village for himself. He wasn't sure why he even wanted to go.

It wasn't that he didn't trust her, he did. It was more that he wanted to say a final goodbye to the place. If it was never rebuilt it would soon return to the earth.

The only thing that would be left was his memory of it.

He climbed the ridge and scrambled down the far side, pushing through the trees until he came out into the open.

The village itself was in a natural amphitheater. To the left was the loch, drifting far north and wide, sparkling in the morning light, the ripples in the wind reminding him of the movement of chainmail just before battle, shimmering and catching the eye.

Around the loch were tall crags of mountains, snowcapped and steep, sprigs of heather creating spots of color here and there but otherwise gray and brown, curlews flying low, swooping over the loch.

He didn't want to look right but he could only look at the water for so long. Finally, taking a deep breath, he turned his head.

He prepared himself mentally as much as he could, but it was still a shock. The village he'd known so well was nothing but a blackened ruin.

The cleansing fire had long burned out. Nothing grew there. The crumbling foundations of few buildings remained amongst the black and gray dead land. It was a place of decay.

And yet there was a flash of color down there. What was that?

He walked down, thinking of the people he'd known when he was younger. There was the baker, Tam and his wife, crossing from Ireland as a bairn, settled thirty years, wee un on the way. All of them gone in the first weeks.

The tailor, red beard and fierce eyes on old Damos, yelling at him every time he passed that he needed to take better care of his tartan, that it brought shame on the clan. Gone.

The children he'd played with. Little Sasha, the oldest of their group, the one he'd had an irredeemable crush on, the one he planned to marry when he hit the ripe old age of five.

Her death had been the first one. She'd been with her father to market and come back talking about a beggar they'd met on their return, how he'd hidden his face but when he held out his hand for alms they'd seen the buboes on his wrist.

It had been too late by then to do anything. She told Tavish but he didn't tell anyone. He kept it to himself. All of this was his fault. If he'd only told his father, they could have isolated Sasha and her father before it was too late, prayed for God to help purify the village.

It was all his fault. He'd killed them all. He almost staggered as he walked down what was the main road to the village green. All dead because of him. No matter what he did to save the clan, he had killed an entire village.

He got closer to the green and had to wipe his eyes before he could see what was there, his vision blurring slightly.

Then he saw it. Kneeling down where the entrance to the chapel had been, he saw it and he knew at once who'd done it.

He turned and marched back out of the village, not stopping for breath before he was back at the house, panting slightly as he marched inside and found her pulling the fish from the spit. "Are you hungry?" she asked.

"Did ye do it?" he asked, ignoring the fish.

"What? Why are you so angry?"

"Answer me. Did ye do it?"

"Do what?"

"The village green. The carving, it was ye wasn't it?"

She blushed, unable to look him in the eye. "You weren't supposed to see that. Are you angry?"

"Angry?" he said, sitting in the chair opposite her. "You placed a carving of my mother with a wreath of bluebells on sacred ground and you think I might be angry?"

"Please, don't be cross. It was just meant to be a tribute to your mom. I know it's weird but when I saw you asleep I had a vision of what she looked like. It was like she was standing right where you are now, so close I could see the coloraturas of her eyes. The carving was easy. I marked it with an S for Sinclair, like the one on the stairs."

He rubbed his eyes, leaning forward, his hand stretching out toward her. She looked down at his hand, looking scared before finally letting him hold it.

"It is the most beautiful tribute I could ever imagine," he said quietly. "Ah thank ye."

He held onto her fingers for another moment before letting go, shutting the emotions down that threatened to bubble up inside him. "Is that fish ready yet?"

"Huh?" she said, blinking as if unsure what he was talking about. "Oh, yes. Here you go."

As they ate he kept stealing glances at her. She'd not only listened to him talking about his mother. She'd carved a tribute to her and to all those who'd died in the village.

Had she known she picked the chapel entrance to lay down the bluebells? No, of course not, that was impossible. All the same, something had guided her there. Quinn was right. There was something special about her.

At that moment he made a vow to himself. He

would not rest for a single moment until he had repaid what she'd done for him. Whatever it might be, whatever it might take, he would repay her for the tribute to his childhood and his home.

Together, they ate their breakfast in silence.

Chapter Nine

The look on Tavish's face told Lindsey everything she needed to know. He was clearly a tough man who had lived a hard life. His gruff exterior hid a depth she hadn't expected.

When she'd first met him he seemed rude and abrupt but that was just on the surface. Underneath was something she hadn't expected.

The miscarriage of justice had almost crushed him but somehow he'd found the strength to keep going, to keep living even when everyone else had given up on him. Behind the pain, there was a boy who'd loved his mother, who'd loved the place where he'd grown up. A boy like any other.

She'd seen the look when he was giving her the

tour of his house, but she hadn't understood it then. She saw it again when he fell into his chair after discovering her carving.

She hadn't whittled the statue for him to find. She'd done it because it seemed like a fitting tribute to his mother and to a village vanished forever. She had no idea who'd lived there but she knew about the plague. Those who died did so in pain and fear.

The bluebell wreath and the carving represented everyone who'd gone, her tiny little tribute to a place and time she would soon be leaving forever. In a way, it was also her thanks to whatever force had brought her back through time, a way of showing her gratitude for what had happened.

She was grateful. Despite nearly drowning and initially thinking a brutish Highlander might kill her, despite the fact she was going to try and sneak into a castle and become a thief for the first time in her life. She was glad it had happened.

She had come back and would be able to do at least one good thing while she was in the Middle Ages in Scotland.

When he'd walked in after finding the carving, she was terrified of him. He no longer looked like the man she'd gotten to know over the last couple of days. He looked like a wild animal.

It took a moment to see past it. When she did, she was able to regain control of herself. She saw the tremble in his lip, the way his eye glistened as he sank into the chair. It wasn't anger, it was something much deeper that was powering him.

Then the truth came out and they had held hands. Although she didn't say it out loud, that was the moment she realized the true reason she was doing this.

It was the same reason why she'd decided to collect the bluebells she saw on the shore of the loch. A small patch of them under an ash tree, no other flowers anywhere to be seen. She looked at them whilst shivering from the effects of cleaning herself in the icy cold water. They spoke to her.

Kneeling down to collect the bluebells, she spotted a lump of wood next to them. It was out of place, looking like a freshly cut log rather than a fallen branch. It was the perfect size for her to carve.

She gathered it up while thinking of working on the Celtic design she'd seen inside Tavish's house. It was while carrying the bluebells into the village that the idea came to her to carve something very different.

She had no idea what Tavish's mother looked

like. And yet when she heard a woman's voice in his room the previous night, she could picture her perfectly.

Flaming red hair, tall, ethereal like an elf queen out of a Tolkien novel. The knife had moved in her hand with little conscious effort of her own, the figure emerging from the wood simply and without any effort.

She left the bluebells with the figure, her little memorial to all that had happened in the past.

She hadn't planned for what would happen if he saw it. She had no clue he would return and end up holding her hand, showing her a softness hidden inside him. The look in his face as his warmth spread into her fingers was everything.

"I brought something with me," she said when they'd finished breakfast, making a decision to share something she never thought she would. "From my time, I mean. Would you like to see?"

He nodded without saying anything, sitting bolt upright in his chair.

She reached into the folds of her cloak and brought out the photos. The water from her near-drowning had damaged them but she had still kept them, fearing they might be her only link to the present if she was unable to get back.

Although the colors had shifted and the images blurred it was still possible to make out the contents. She handed them to Tavish.

"What are these?" he asked, examining them closely. "Is this…is this ma hoose?"

She nodded. "We took them on a Polaroid camera when mom first got the place. Look, that's her with the key."

He stared in shock at the photos, touching the paper as if he thought they might come to life. He smiled. "She's laughing. Why is she laughing?"

"Because she was given a key but there's no front door left."

He looked closer at the picture. "You look like her."

"Do you think so?"

"Aye. I never knew what my mother looked like." He handed the photos back, his fingers lingering on hers for a moment. "Ah could only wish for something such as that. How do you create a drawing so lifelike? It's like witchcraft."

"It's not witchcraft. It's…" She paused, realizing she had no idea how a camera actually worked. "It's complicated but it's not witchcraft."

"Why are you showing me these?"

"Because you had a mom same as me. I want

you to see mine and to know I want more than anything to make your house look like it does now to make both of you happy."

"What? Have it filled with weeds and dust?"

She laughed. "No, filled with life. With a proper roof and walls and those Celtic marks your grandfather made."

"What for?"

"To remember you when I go back."

"Because I'm dead in your time, I ken." His voice was quieter than before. "'Tis strange to think of a world so far in the future yet so nearby."

She put the photos away again. It wasn't quite the reaction she'd been expecting but then she had somehow not been able to say what she wanted.

She wanted him to see she had nothing to hide, no secrets she was keeping, no matter how small. She trusted him and wanted him to trust her. He had hidden the locket when he hadn't had to, he had looked after her from the moment she'd arrived in the Highlands.

She wanted to tell him something she was keeping to herself and that had been the perfect moment to do it but now the moment had passed and instead she'd talked about doing up the house. She'd been able to introduce him to her mother, in a sense, but she hadn't been able to say the one thing she wanted to.

"Come on," he said, getting out of the chair and crossing to the doorway. "Before our steed decides to make his own way to MacIntyre Castle."

Later that day Lindsey encountered real penury, the kind she had never seen in her life. She and her mom might have been short of cash at times, but nothing could have prepared her for the wretched hovel they passed in the late afternoon.

They'd just about worked their way through a broad valley surrounded by thin looking cattle and come out the other side to waste. The ground here was unused, no farms or signs of life anywhere.

They were high above sea level having gradually climbed for most of the day. Surrounding them in the distance were high mountains that cast the valley into shadow. At the far end of the valley, the land began to rise again.

Halfway up the hill, there was a glen that dipped toward a small pond. Beside it was a tumbledown building that looked one stiff breeze away from collapse.

At first, Lindsey thought the hovel was abandoned but then she heard a crying baby from inside. "We have to stop," she said.

"Why?" Tavish grunted behind her.

"It might be alone in there."

He didn't say anything else, but he did turn the horse off the trail and toward the building. The nearer they got the more Lindsey's nose began to wrinkle.

The smell rising from the place was awful. The stones were crumbling, rotten wood all that was holding up the roof of moldy straw. The baby's cry continued as she slid from the horse and ran to the door, knocking loudly. "Anyone in?"

It opened at once, sending a darker smell out that was so strong she staggered back. From the gloom inside a figure emerged, a wraith, so thin her bones were visible through her ragged clothes.

"We've nothing to steal," the figure said, not looking Lindsey in the eye. "Be on your way."

A second figure emerged, leaning heavily on the doorframe. "Whit dae ye want?" It was a man, skin so pale it was almost see-through, eyes watering as he stared through her into the distance. Was he blind?

"Have you anything for the bairn?" the woman asked. "She starves and the crop was burned by the MacIntyre laird. They took ma husband's eyes and all the food we had. Please, I beg you, help us."

"Wait there," Lindsey said, running back to Tavish who was still sitting on the horse. "We have to go back," she said.

"What? Go back where? To the well?"

"Not the well, your house."

"Why? What for?"

"To get the locket." She was managing to hold back her tears but only just. "They need it."

"Here," he said, climbing down from the horse and slipping something into her hand, folding her fingers over it.

She looked down as he moved away. In her palm was a heavy gold coin. She ran back to the house. The man had vanished back inside. Lindsey could hear him attempting to shush the baby. "Take this," she said, pressing the coin into the woman's hand.

"And this," a voice said behind her. She turned to see Tavish standing next to the horse. He looked at her and shrugged. "We're nearly there, we can walk the rest of the way." He spoke in a clear voice as he turned to the woman. "Take this beast and ride with your bairn to Castle Sinclair. Tell them Tavish will return with the sacred stone. They will feed you and your child for a lifetime in return for such news."

The woman was still staring down at her hand as if she thought she might be dreaming. "This is more than ah've seen in ma life," she said quietly. "I cannae take it. It is too much."

"Ah willnae take it back," Tavish said. "Leave the MacIntyres to their fate and take yours in your hands as we do our own. Come, while the light lasts. Get on."

Lindsey stood to one side, watching as Tavish carried the baby out of the hovel. He held it while the man dragged himself up onto the horse.

It was hard to see people living like this. She'd read of Highlanders starving to death during the wars between the clans but this was the reality of it. Death leaning on the shoulders of three people who deserved so much more.

She wept quietly as she watched the man take the baby while Tavish helped the woman onto the horse.

"God protect you," the man said as Tavish whispered into the long ear of their steed. The horse listened, understanding every word before turning and heading back south.

Lindsey wiped her eyes before Tavish reached her. "Ye must walk the rest of the way," he said.

She threw her arms around him and burst into

fresh tears. "Thank you," she said into his shoulder.

His arms held her tight while she cried until she could cry no more. "I've never seen anything like that," she said when the tears finally began to ease.

"The war brings hardship upon those who can least bear it," he replied. His hands were still on her back, their faces inches apart.

"You are a good person, Tavish," she said quietly, blinking up at him, feeling his hand in the small of her back.

She could feel his breath on her cheek. He looked as if he might be about to kiss her but then he didn't, pulling away.

"Time is short," he said. "And without a steed, we must make haste if we are to reach MacIntyre Castle by tomorrow."

"We are that close?"

"Aye. One more night's rest and we'll be there. Home to those that would blind old men and burn crops out of nothing but spite."

That night Lindsey was glad to stop. They had marched long into the dark, settling deep in a wood where there was little risk of being seen. As she sat rubbing her aching feet, Tavish strung together a basic shelter made of leaves and branches.

Though it looked little better than sleeping in

the open Lindsey was surprised when she climbed inside. It was roomy, warm, and kept out the night chill far better than she expected.

"It's so warm," she said, making space for Tavish to lay down next to her.

"Lots of leaves under you," he replied as if that explained everything.

"You did a good thing today," she said, reaching out to touch his shoulder in the darkness.

"As did you," he replied, leaning up and squeezing her hand. "Ah wouldnae have stopped."

They lay together in the darkness as outside an owl hooted loudly and then a twig snapped. Lindsey shuddered without knowing why. Before she knew what was happening Tavish had taken her into the cruck of his arm, holding her close to him.

"What was that?" she asked, the sound of rustling growing closer.

"You are safe," he replied. "I will let nothing hurt you."

"But something's out there."

"It's only a boar and he's after truffles, not you."

"How can you tell?"

"I can smell him. Listen, he moves away."

The rustling sound died but Lindsey remained where she was, her head on Tavish's chest. Her eyes began to close. There was something warm and comforting about hearing his heartbeat, slow and steady compared to her own pounding thud.

She was no sooner asleep than she was at home. She stood beside her mother who was tapping her foot, trying to ignore a hammering on the front door.

"Open up," a gruff voice was shouting. "You can't hide in there forever."

"I'm game," Rhona shouted back. "Let's see who gets bored first."

"We're going to repossess whether you like it or not, Mrs. MacMillan. You have to let us in."

Another voice beside the first. "You owe us. Open up."

"Mom," Lindsey said, reaching out to tap her mom on the shoulder. Her hand passed straight through and her mom became nothing more but mist. The sound of hammering fists on wood continued but fainter, eventually fading into silence.

"Shush, just a bad dream." Tavish's voice, quiet, his hand stroking her forehead.

She lay still, no longer sure what was a dream and what was real. His hand was comforting and she yearned for him to kiss her. It made her whole body ache with desire but she said nothing.

She mustn't allow herself to get too close to him. She had to concentrate. Getting distracted by falling for him was a bad idea. She'd end up staying here if he felt the same and that was what the dream was trying to remind her. She needed to focus on what mattered.

If she fell in love and he felt the same she still had to go home. Otherwise, her mom wouldn't know where the locket was. The repossession would still go ahead, and she'd be homeless, living on the streets, never knowing what happened to her daughter.

Not that it mattered. He'd shown no signs of wanting to kiss her. She was reading too much into him comforting her as they lay together. He was just trying to calm her fears, that was all.

She rolled away from Tavish, pretending she was still asleep, hearing nothing else from him other than a slight rustle of the leaves that served as his bed.

She had agreed to do this, and she would. She would get the stone to help him, but she would not fall for him. It could never work. He was a loner anyway, used to being on his own.

He might have looked like he was going to kiss her, but she'd hugged him, not the other way around. She'd probably just read too much into things.

The swirling doubt in her mind felt like the mist in the dream. She settled back into an uneasy sleep, hoping to speak to her mother again, tell her she was coming home.

She did not dream for the rest of the night. Seven hundred years in the future Rhona MacMillan awoke in the middle of the night to a strange tingling feeling on her shoulder as if it had just been touched by someone.

She was so sure Lindsey had been standing right there behind her but of course, she wasn't. She was still on vacation at Loch Tay, hopefully meeting a nice man somewhere and having a great time.

She had quite the story to tell her when she got back. Her boss was in trouble with the tax office. Someone might have rung them to suggest they look into his habit of banking staff tips for himself.

The story had ended up in the paper. Cafe owner under investigation. It might not go anywhere but then again maybe he'd start paying his staff properly.

Rhona settled again. That story could wait until Lindsey got back. For now, let her enjoy herself.

Chapter Ten

T he castle came into view in the early afternoon. Tavish had brought them up a craggy outcrop of rock that circled the side of a mountain. There had been few signs of life since they'd set off that morning.

His fear about being caught had subsided once they'd left the main track and made their way through short grass to the loch that marked the first natural defense of MacIntyre Castle. Skirting that brought them closer.

He'd not been this near since the last war and that had been a long time ago, a year before his exile. He'd barely been a boy when he'd seen his first real battle. So much death. So many screams.

The higher they climbed, the more thoughts fell

away until he was back in the role he knew well, scouting an entrenched enemy position.

"There," he said, laying down and crawling forward until he could peer over the far side of the ridge.

Halfway down the other side, the mountain had suffered a rockfall eons ago. Whatever had caused it had scoured the side of the cliff, gouging a line down to the valley floor. The fallen rubble had been used to build the castle that sat hidden in the valley.

When he'd first studied the other clans, he'd thought only a fool would build a castle in a valley compared to a hilltop. They couldn't tell if an army were approaching until it would be too late.

He'd soon learned that, like so many things in life, it wasn't quite that simple. There was only one entrance to the valley and that was heavily guarded. No army on horseback could get up or down the sheer cliffs of the surrounding mountains.

That combined with a few well-placed scouts by beacons overlooking the surrounding Highlands was enough to ensure MacIntyre Castle was the only one he knew that had never been successfully besieged.

He'd been part of the army that had tried,

desperately fighting to retrieve the sacred stone of the Sinclair Clan.

"Have you been here before?" Lindsey asked, lying next to him and peering down at the dark stone of the castle.

"Aye, and watched many good men go into that bottleneck in the canyon down there. We didn't get within a quarter of a mile of the place. Arrows rained down from there and there. It was a slaughter."

"Great. So how do I get in?"

"You're not an army. You sneak in up the garderobe."

"Garderobe? You mean the toilet?"

"I dinnae ken that word."

"Never mind. How do I get in a castle through a garderobe?"

"The drop from them tae the gong scourers heap is never guarded. You go in the way the waste goes out."

"You're serious?" She looked scared, glancing from him to the castle and back again.

He crawled back from the edge, beckoning for her to follow. Once the castle was out of sight he sat up.

"Ah will distract the guards overlooking the rear

of the castle. Ye get to the chute at the far corner and get up inside."

"Then what?"

"Then you make your way to the chapel. It shouldnae be hard to find. If ah ken the MacIntyres, they'll have the stone in there somewhere. Wi' any luck, you'll no encounter any trouble. Get the stone and come back out the way ye went in. Ye ken?"

"I think so," she said.

"What is it? Something troubles ye. Are ye too scared?"

"No, it's not that."

"What is it then?"

She sighed, looking up at the sky while picking at the bobbles forming on her cloak. "It's just my mom. What if I get killed? She'll never know what happened to me. She'll think I just walked out on her for no reason."

"She'll have the locket."

"How will she know where it is if I don't survive to go back and tell her?"

"Ah'll find a way tae get a message tae her."

"How?"

"I dinnae ken but I'll figure it out while you're

in the castle. But dinnae worry, lass. You willnae get killed."

"How do you know that? They might shoot an arrow through my heart and mom might never see me again." She was shifting in place, still not looking at him.

He put a finger to her cheek, turning her face gently until she was facing him, her body finally becoming still.

"You will survive," he said, staring deep into her eyes. "You came back seven hundred years for a reason and if this isnae it then I dinnae ken what else it might be. An hour's time we will be heading south with all this behind us."

"But-"

He pressed a finger to her lips. "Dinnae talk no more." He couldn't resist leaning closer. His head had been filled with thoughts of taking her back home, giving up on this fool's errand. With his face an inch from hers those thoughts fell away and all he could do was think how soft her lips looked.

He could smell her body, the sweetness and purity he'd long forgotten existed. He felt her breathing, fast at first but then slowing. Her eyes closed as if she knew what he was going to do before he did.

"Ye will live," he said. Then he kissed her.

There was not a single sound to be heard anywhere around them. The world no longer existed. For the briefest of moments, everything felt perfect. Then she pulled away from him.

She returned to the vantage point and again looked down at the castle. He joined her, saying nothing.

"If I die," she said, not looking at him, "find a way to tell her what happened to me."

"I will," he replied.

She was on her feet a second later. "Better get that diversion ready. If I wait any longer, I won't be able to do it."

Her hands were shaking as she slowly began to climb down the rocky escarpment toward the castle.

There wasn't time to think about the kiss. She was already moving faster than he'd anticipated.

He crouched low and ran toward the guard post about a quarter of a mile to his left. As he approached it, he calculated his odds.

One guard asleep slumped against the side of the beacon. His torch was lit ready to fire up the warning to the clan but it was about ten feet from him, wedged between two tall rocks, the flames flickering in the breeze.

The other guard was looking down into the valley. Had he spotted Lindsey?

Without stopping to think Tavish crossed the space to the outpost, leaping over the sleeping guard and landing silently behind the other one who was staring at Lindsey. Tavish had seconds to act.

He got his arms around the throat of the guard, catching him before he could say a word to his companion. Squeezing his arms, he was rewarded by the gasping breaths of the man who fought ineffectually to free himself from the vice-like grip of his attacker.

Tavish didn't let go for a second as they fell back, the guard slumping to his knees then finally onto his face.

He was unconscious, not dead. Tavish had no wish for bloodshed unless absolutely necessary, not even with a MacIntyre. The sleeping guard still had not stirred.

Tavish moved to the torch, grabbing it and tossing it away, making sure the beacon could not be lit any time soon. When that was done he edged toward the prone figure on the woolen blanket, kneeling beside him and whistling loudly.

The guard stirred and as he began to sit up,

Tavish got him around the neck, staring into the furious eyes of a much stronger man than the first.

He was forced back, the guard reaching for his sword. Tavish stretched out an arm and got to it first, tossing it down the mountainside.

The two of them stumbled into the iron cradle that held the beacon, kindling and dust falling into his face as they rolled sideways, coming ever closer to the edge of the ridge. He found himself on the rim a moment later, looking down at a fall of at least fifty feet.

"You're dead," the guard snarled, pushing him further over, trying to use brute force to send him to his doom.

Tavish glanced down, seeing Lindsey looking back up at him from far away. Seeing the look in her eyes gave him strength and with a grunt and a monumental heave of his arms, he managed to shove the guard away.

The guard leaned down and scooped up his sword. Tavish went for his own and a second later the two blades crashed together. The guard was fast, jabbing continually, pushing Tavish back once again toward the edge of the ridge.

He felt his feet slipping from him, stones clattering down over the rim and disappearing down the mountainside. The guard let out a laugh.

"You're Tavish Sinclair," he said, jabbing once again as Tavish visibly sagged in place, almost tumbling and barely managing to keep his balance. "They said you were the best fighter in the Highlands. You're nothing but a washed-up murderer."

"Aye," replied Tavish. "But I'm something else as well."

"What's that?" the guard asked, pushing forward with the final lunge that would send Tavish to his death.

"Quick on my feet." Tavish leaped to the side, flicking his sword into the hilt of his opponent's, flinging it loose from his grip and sending it clattering down into the abyss. The guard almost fell after it but Tavish caught him at the last second, getting his hands around the man's throat and choking him into unconsciousness in seconds.

He tugged the sagging figure back from the edge, laying him by his companion before pausing to wipe the sweat from his brow. Looking down at the castle he could no longer see Lindsey. All he could do was wait to see if she emerged.

It was the longest wait of his life. The guards were bound and gagged with their own tartans.

He'd deliberately used loose knots. They'd get themselves free in a couple of hours but by then he'd be long gone with the stone.

Crouching at the spot where she'd headed down, he craned his neck in the hope of seeing her. He couldn't help but think about the kiss.

It had been a foolish thing to do and he had learned his lesson. He would not attempt such a thing again. He did not even know why he'd done it.

He couldn't ask her. To do so would embarrass them both. She would try not to hurt his feelings but the fact of the matter was clear. No matter if she felt true love for him, she still had to get back to her own time where she belonged.

He should try and erase the kiss from his memory, pretend it never happened. She'd probably already erased it, he just needed to do the same.

That was easier said than done when he had gained the knowledge of just how soft her lips were.

An hour passed and in that time he decided he would never mention the kiss, nor his growing feelings for her. It would only cause pain for him and embarrassment for her to do so. She was going home and that was clearly what mattered to her, not the feelings of a banished member of a failing clan.

He lay perfectly still, praying for her safety, asking the Lord for His help in bringing her back to him. His desire for the stone had gone. All he wanted was for her to get out of there alive. If she died it would be his fault. He had sent her into the lion's den with no protection.

Fear rose up in him that she had already been caught. Another hour rolled by and he tried to prepare himself for the worst. She wasn't coming out.

She'd probably gone in there and told them where he was, told them who he was. Any minute the castle gates would open and an army would come out to collect him for execution.

The castle gates rolled open and he winced. There was no point running. They knew this land far better than him and there was nowhere to hide this high up. Someone was down there, a figure emerging from the castle. It was her. She was waving, beckoning him to come down and join her.

Chapter Eleven

❧

L indsey couldn't stop thinking about the kiss as she clambered down the side of the mountain toward the castle, doing her best to concentrate on what she was about to do.

Her lips continued to tingle, making it impossible for her to forget what had just happened. It had come from nowhere.

She never thought in her wildest dreams that Tavish had any intention of kissing her. Whenever he seemed to warm to her, he closed down again and she'd given up trying to understand why. Then, out of nowhere, he just did it.

She'd heard that kisses could be more than just kisses. She didn't believe it until it had happened to her. She'd only been kissed once and that was

Bobby Tucker doing it for a bet when she was fourteen and the only girl in school with braces.

Nothing in her life had led her to believe that a kiss could send her stomach cartwheeling up to bump into her heart which was thudding hard enough to burst out of her chest. Her whole body trembled the moment their lips pressed together and she had to fight like she was escaping quicksand to end it.

It had to stop. She knew that. But it was like trying to just have one piece of chocolate and wrapping up the rest of the bar. She knew perfectly well that kissing him was a bad idea. One kiss and she wanted much more.

Pulling away from that kiss was the hardest thing she'd ever had to do in her life, but she had no choice. If he was going back to his clan and she was going back to her mom, they couldn't go any further down that dangerous road.

At the end was love and she wasn't ever going to go there. It would only end in pain when she had to say goodbye. Far better to let that one kiss linger in her memory. She was going home. She must not fall for him.

The way he switched back to talking about their plan proved he wasn't that bothered anyway. She made her way down from the ridge telling herself to ignore how she felt, to ignore the fireworks that had gone off when their lips touched, to focus on what mattered. Getting the sacred stone and then getting home.

When she heard fighting above her, she looked up, seeing him on the verge of falling to his death. A moment later he had the upper hand and the man he was fighting was falling from view.

She turned away. That was who he was. He wasn't a soft and gentle man. He was a Highland brute like the rest of them. She had promised to get the stone and she would, but she would not fall for someone like that. No way.

She found the garderobe entrance just where he'd said it would be. No one was looking down from the battlements. She was able to examine the hole in detail. It was surrounded by filth, the stench enough to make her retch several times while she tried to build up the courage to climb inside.

Glancing around her, she saw a clump of straggly trees beside a fisherman's hut. At once, she thought of Tavish, of how they'd first met.

Stop it, she told herself. It was not the time for reminiscing. Linen had been draped over the branches of the trees to dry. She glanced around her to see if anyone was looking before grabbing the nearest length. Wrapping it around her, she returned to the castle looking like an Egyptian mummy.

"You can do this," she whispered, taking a deep breath before ducking down and pushing her way into the hole in the stone. The smell was far stronger inside and she had to fight for breath as she squeezed her way up the narrow chute, the linen soon soaked through with filth.

After a few feet of climbing, the walls became smoother and she found herself sliding back down. Only by digging her elbows into the stone could she arrest her descent.

Pausing to catch her breath she looked up and down. Eight or so feet from the ground. Another twenty at least left to climb.

Pushing her feet against the far wall, she was able to clamber again, steadily making progress, the hole above her growing closer. She had no idea how long it took.

Several times she slid back until for each foot of progress, she was falling back six inches. Finally, her lungs burning and her limbs on fire from the effort, she got her arms to the hole that opened out into the garderobe chamber high up in the castle.

Using the last of her strength, she yanked herself out, falling in an exhausted heap to the floor, panting for breath.

As soon as she could move again, she unpeeled the length of linen from around her body, tossing it back down the garderobe chute with a grimace. A second later she cursed herself. She'd have to climb back down without its protection.

It was too late to worry about that. She needed to move before she was spotted. The garderobe had two right angles to it, keeping it shielded from the main chamber beyond.

She edged along, peering through a thick curtain into a solar. There was no one in view but she had to stop for a moment to take in the beauty of the sight before her.

She'd been in many medieval castles in her time but they were recreations of how they might have looked. This one was real and it was stunning. The walls were whitewashed and covered in intricate tapestries depicting battle scenes.

The floor was covered with sheepskin rugs, the fireplace dark wood and carved with animals, both real and imagined. Whoever had carved it had done an excellent job.

She crossed the floor to it, able to envision the

craftsman chipping away until the lamb being chased by the fox looked so real it might flick its tail toward her at any moment.

From the window, she could hear noise. She darted across to glance out. There was plenty of life down there and again she had to pause to admire it. She was seeing something no one from her time would ever get a chance to see.

The sound of hammering came from a forge in the corner, a blacksmith at work on a sword, surrounded by billowing smoke. Further on a group of women in dresses of vivid green were at work on small looms. Dogs ran about, children darted to and fro. Tartan-clad men marched back and forth. The place was a buzz of activity.

There was the chapel, not far from where she was. How to get to it? The answer came at once. All she had to do was look busy. There were so many people there, who would spot one more?

Turning away from the window she headed downstairs, pushing open the door at the bottom and stepping out into the courtyard.

She kept her hood up, hoping no one would notice one more figure. Those who saw her gave her a wide berth, the smell of the garderobe lingering upon her.

She tried to keep calm and walk normally but her limbs seemed to have other ideas.

"Just relax," she muttered, concentrating on slowing her breathing, trying not to stand out at all.

She kept her eyes fixed in front of her, not stopping as she weaved between the people before reaching the chapel. She ducked inside, pushing the door closed behind her before letting out a sigh of relief.

Tavish hadn't told her what the stone looked like, she realized as she looked about her. How was she supposed to know if she found it?

He'd said to look by the altar, hadn't he?

The altar was simple, a single long stone slab supported on two thick stumps of wood. Between the stumps was a wooden box and something told her to look inside. As she opened it she smiled. Inside was a small square of stone about six inches in diameter. In the middle was carved an S in the same Celtic design she'd seen in Tavish's house.

"You've come for the stone," a voice said behind her as she ran her finger along the curves of the S.

Leaping up in fright, she slammed her head into the base of the altar stone, staggering to her feet, the hood of her cloak slipping from her face.

She found herself looking at a blurred man who

had somehow walked into the chapel without making a sound.

"Wh-" she said, stumbling to her knees, dizziness washing over her.

"Apothecary," the figure shouted. "In the chapel with haste."

Another figure appeared beside the first and the two of them walked toward Lindsey while she tried to scramble away from them. They came into focus when they reached her.

"Do not fear," the nearest man said, "We mean you no harm."

"Who are you?" the second asked. "Are you hurt?"

"I just banged my head," she replied, her voice weak.

"Punishment enough for sneaking into my castle," the first man said, chuckling to himself.

Lindsey let them help her up, looking at them both closely. "Who are you?"

The first man spoke. "I am Dom MacIntyre, laird of the clan. This is Father Adam, apothecary and builder of this chapel. And you are?"

"Lindsey MacMillan."

"Of clan MacMillan? What brings you so far north?"

"It's a long story and I'm not sure you'd believe me."

"We love long stories here and we have all the time in the world to listen. Speak."

Lindsey found herself telling them the truth. Later, she wondered why she'd done it. She guessed it was the blow to her head making her feel woozy. It might have been the quiet serenity of the chapel, the very air telling her she was safe there. It might have just been the warm smiles on the two people sitting with her.

It was hard to square the way they were with her knowledge of the pauper family they'd passed on their way north. This laird seemed kind, ensuring kitchen maids brought her hot drinks while she talked and talked and talked.

When she mentioned coming from the future, the two of them looked at each other, whispering something she didn't catch.

She told them about arriving, about finding Tavish, about his banishment from the clan. She felt no qualms in telling them she had come north to retrieve the sacred stone.

When she was finished the two of them were silent for a moment before the laird took her hand. "You were meant to come to us," he said. "Isn't that right, Father?"

"God has guided her here through the ages as He did the others, praise the Lord."

"I must say something else," Lindsey said. "On the way here, we passed a family in the depths of poverty. They said you had burned their crops. Why would you do such a thing?"

The laird shook his head sadly. "That was my father. A cruel man, I am afraid. Times are different now I'm in charge, not that the Sinclairs could yet know the lairdship has changed hands. I seek only peace with all the clans of the Highlands.

"Edward is coming north with his army or so rumor has it. If we are to repel him, we must work together, not bicker amongst ourselves. If you would go to Castle Sinclair and return with an emissary of peace, I will gladly give you their sacred stone in turn as a gesture of good faith."

"I have an emissary outside right now."

"Really, who?"

"Tavish."

The laird shook his head. "We cannot talk peace with an exiled murderer."

"Did you not hear me just now? He is guilty of no crime."

"Nonetheless, the Sinclairs will not listen to him so nor can we."

The apothecary spoke up. "That is why she wants the stone. So that they can gain entry to Castle Sinclair and prove his innocence. Do you see?"

The laird turned to his companion. "You are right as ever, Father." He turned back to Lindsey. "Prove the truth of which you speak. Bring Tavish to me and I will gladly give you the stone to take back to its rightful home. Perhaps then we may unite as a single people as has always been my wish."

A minute later, Lindsey was standing waving outside the castle gate, hoping Tavish was watching from his vantage point. She was rewarded by the sight of a figure standing up, silhouetted against the sky for a brief moment before beginning the descent to her.

"What happened?" he asked when he reached her a few minutes later. "Do you have the stone?"

"Come with me," she replied, taking his hand and leading him into the castle. "There is someone who wishes to meet you."

Tavish looked utterly bewildered as he walked beside her into the castle. People stopped what they were doing when they saw him, muttering to each other and pointing at the outlaw.

"Tavish Sinclair," the laird called out from the steps of the keep. "You are most welcome. Come, break bread with me."

"Am I dreaming?" Tavish whispered to Lindsey as they climbed the steps to follow the laird inside.

A minute later the three of them were sitting at a small round table, trenchers and goblets in front of each of them. "This is a remarkable woman," Dom said, nodding toward Lindsey. "You'd do well to look after her."

"I intend to. But where is the laird?"

"Dead these six weeks. I am laird now."

"I am most sorry for the loss of your father."

"I'm not. He was a wicked man and the cause of much bloodshed between our two clans. But let us put that behind us. I have an offer for you, Tavish Sinclair."

Tavish tore off a hunk of bread and ate it slowly. Lindsey watched as the laird did the same, the two men examining each other closely.

Finally, the laird burst into laughter. "You are a strong man but your eyes betray you. I see you want peace as much as me. Take the sacred stone and return to Castle Sinclair. Send them my blessing and ask for parley. We must have peace between the clans if we are to avoid a bloody future."

Tavish twisted in his seat, giving Lindsey a look she understood at once.

"I told him the truth," she said. "He knows I'm from the future."

The laird slid a red velvet bag across the table. "The sacred stone, blessed by our holy men, given freely by the laird of the MacIntyres to you, emissary of the Sinclairs. Take it and fresh horses with all the food you need for your journey home."

"I cannot ride," Lindsey said. "Though I thank you for your gift."

"Ride together on one then," the laird replied, his smile not fading. "You look like neither of you will find that too great a discomfort."

He got to his feet, holding a hand out toward Tavish who looked at it for several seconds whilst saying nothing. Then he too rose to his feet.

"Peace," he said, shaking firmly.

"Peace," the laird replied. "Lindsey, I have fresh clothes to replace those if you desire. They are somewhat ripe."

"Very much so," Lindsey replied.

She changed in a side-room, listening as Tavish and the laird talked about what rumors were spreading regarding the English king. Once she was changed, she walked back out to find both men on their feet.

The laird turned to her. "Now you should both make haste. Your companion tells me you wish to free your father from captivity."

"Aye," Tavish said, picking up the velvet bag before turning to Lindsey. "Ready, lass?"

"I am," she replied.

The laird took them to the stable. "This is a fine beast," he said, slapping a black horse on the flank. "Name of Dom after me. He will serve you well. God speed Tavish Sinclair and may you safely return to your home, Lindsey MacMillan."

"Farewell," Tavish said, helping Lindsey onto the horse before climbing up behind her.

"Goodbye," Lindsey called over her shoulder as they rode through the courtyard. Behind her, the laird and apothecary waved until they were out of sight.

"I can't believe you did that," Tavish said, leaning forward and kissing her forehead before laughing properly for the first time in days. "You just walked intae MacIntyre castle and retrieved the stone without even breaking intae a sweat."

"I don't know about that," she replied, trying to

ignore the tingle running up the back of her spine. "The climb up the garderobe wasn't exactly a walk in the park."

"We have the stone," Tavish said. "Ah can go home at last."

Lindsey winced. She hadn't thought about it for some time but he had just reminded her. She was going home too. Her time with Tavish Sinclair was almost at an end.

All she would have to remember him was a kiss and a locket. It would have to do. She had warned herself not to get too close. It was her own fault if this hurt. The kiss meant far more to her than to him. That was clear. He didn't seem bothered in the slightest that she was going.

She had done what she'd promised. It was time to go back to where she belonged. Put all this behind her. Get the locket, quit her job, put her all into doing up the house with her mother. That was what mattered, not the smell and heat coming from the man mountain on the horse behind her, her arm around her waist, making her feel so safe she could cry.

Chapter Twelve

The journey south took many days but for Tavish, it felt as if it were over in minutes. As each mile passed by, he found himself again and again trying to imagine life without Lindsey.

He wasn't sure why he was struggling so much. It was always going to end this way. He'd manipulated her into helping him get the sacred stone and then she could go back to her own time.

They stopped for the last night together on the shore of Loch Tay. The sun set while they sat together eating rabbit like they'd done on the day she arrived in his time.

His tiny little hut was behind them, the last rays

of the evening sun sliding down its walls to the ground. Soon it would be dark and the hut would be hidden from view, as would she.

She was watching the sun set over the water. He looked at her closely, trying to work out what she was thinking. She'd barely said two words to him all day.

Something had changed during their ride south and he couldn't put his finger on it. Whenever he'd asked her what was wrong, she insisted she was fine.

Perhaps she was having the same doubts as him.

He still had a long way to go. The stone might get him into Castle Sinclair but Lilias could still stick to her story. He would continue to live under the burden of suspicion even if his exile were overturned for retrieving the stone.

He needed to work out what he was going to do but he couldn't make himself think that far ahead. All he could think about was the fact that in the morning Lindsey would be back in her own time and he would be alone again.

No longer feeling hungry, he dropped his skewer of meat to the floor. What did it matter about being alone? He was perfectly content with being alone before she came along. He could do it again. No problem.

"Are you cold?" he asked, getting to his feet. "Ah'll top up the fire?"

"I'm fine," she replied without looking at him.

The stone in its velvet bag was on the ground beside her. She had her hand on top of it and he suddenly had the strangest fear that she might throw it into the loch.

Instead, she turned and looked at him, her face pale. "I don't know what to do," she said.

"About what," he replied, reaching out to take her hand. She looked at it but didn't move.

"You should look happier, you've got the stone. You can go home at last." Her voice fell to little more than a whisper. "And so should I."

He couldn't keep quiet any longer. "Stay," he said, putting his hand on top of hers. "Stay with me."

She looked down at his hand, her shoulders sagging. Without looking up, she said, "I want to but I can't."

"Why can ye not?"

"I don't belong here."

"Ye do, lass. You've brought peace between the MacIntyres and the Sinclairs. Do ye ken how long we've been fighting? Since long before ah were born."

She looked up at him, pulling her hands to her chest, folding her arms. "I've got to go back."

"Ye dinnae mean that. I can tell just by looking at you. You want tae stay. Ah ken it so why cannae ye?"

"It's not that simple though is it? My mom will think I've gone missing. She'll never know what happened to me if I don't go back. And what about the locket, how will she know where to find it? I have to tell her."

"I said I'd think of a way to let her know where it is."

"And?"

"I havenae thought of it yet but ah will. Dinnae go."

She shivered as a breeze began to blow across the loch. "I don't know what to do," she said quietly to herself more than him.

"Sleep on it," he replied. "Ah've lit a blaze inside. Let the campfire die. Ye may feel different in the morning. This place has a way of speaking tae people while they sleep."

Getting to his feet, he waited for her to stand up. Her eyes were twinkling in the light of the campfire. She looked more beautiful than ever.

"Whatever ye decide, ah will respect," he said before turning and heading into the hut.

He'd laid out two beds of straw inside, piling woolen blankets on hers to better keep out the chill of the night.

"Goodnight, lass," he said as she lay down and rolled the other way to face the wall.

She didn't reply.

He headed outside, tamping down the last of the fire. He sat for a moment behind the embers, breathing in the thick smoke while looking out at the water. Mist would come in the morning. He could feel it in his bones.

She had come out of the mist. Would she leave the same way? Fading from view until he was left with nothing but memories.

If only he could think of a way of getting a message to her mother.

He leaned back, his hand falling onto the velvet bag containing the stone. He should be happy. His exile was almost over. They had retrieved the stone. The clan would be all the stronger for it.

A few weeks ago he would never have thought it possible. He was about to go home. The biggest problem was what kind of home would it be if she wasn't there by his side?

Making his way back inside, he could tell she was dreaming, her body shifting in place. She looked in pain, moaning quietly.

He knelt beside her, placing his hand on her forehead for what might be the last time. "Shush, lass," he said quietly. "Ah will let nothing harm ye."

She moved onto her back, the groans dying away as she fell still. Once he was sure she was at peace, he moved across to his bed and lay down.

It was a long time before he slept, his eyes wide open in the darkness as he tried to shake the emotions coursing through him. He'd lived without a woman for a long time. He could do it again. He would survive.

In that moment he had an epiphany. Though he had never done so before, he knew he was in love. For the first time in his life, he could see himself marrying, having children, having a family. All with her.

He'd never thought about it before, never given it as much as a moment of his time.

Now, things were different. He lay down with a smile on his lips. He loved her. In the morning he would tell her.

When he woke up, he rolled onto his side and opened his eyes. Her bed was empty.

He was up a second later, running outside and calling her name. She was nowhere to be seen. Mist swirled over the surface of the loch. The water was still. It reflected the red and orange of the sky, the view stunning. He didn't care. Where was she?

Far out on the water, beyond the island, he heard a faint splash. There. Squinting, he ran along the shore until he could see what it was. A rowing boat heading for the island.

She'd walked all the way around the loch to collect it while he'd slept and he hadn't even noticed she'd gone. When had she set off? How had he not heard her go?

He dived in a second later, swimming as fast as he could toward her.

He cut through the water quickly but she had a head start, getting to the island first. When he reached the shore, she was already by the well, pacing around it, trying to work out what to do next.

"Lindsey," he called out, running through the heather to her. "What are ye doing?"

"I've got to go," she said. "How do I do it? You said I can go back if I reach the well. Show me how."

"Will ye stop for a minute and let me talk to ye?"

"No," she snapped, turning to face him. "I saw my mom last night. She's been evicted. They threw her out onto the streets and the locket's right there waiting for her to find it. I need to go."

"What do ye mean you saw her? She came here?"

"I saw it in my sleep. I was back home and I saw her. I never should have left her. This is all my fault, getting distracted by you and this stupid place."

"Look, I've got something I need to tell you."

"I don't want to hear it. You've got your stone, you can go and put your life back together. I need to go home."

"Let me help you." He reached out toward her but she pushed him away. "Ah ken how ye can get in touch-"

She waved a finger at him. "This is all your fault. You took me away from her."

"I'm sure she's fine. It was only a dream."

"You said yourself this place has a way of showing the truth in dreams."

"Listen tae yourself. You dinnae ken what you're saying."

"I know exactly what I'm saying. You only wanted my help so you could get back into your clan and I was stupid enough to help when I should have been helping mom.

"Go, go on. Get out of here. You have what you wanted, you don't need me anymore. Go and live up the good life. I'll work out how to get home by myself."

"Ye need me tae show you what tae dae."

"I'm sure I'll do just fine on my own. And you can take your rowing boat too, I won't need that anymore. I'm going back home where I belong."

"Lindsey-"

"Go!" She shoved him in the chest. "Leave me alone."

Her eyes were cold. He turned without another word, dragging the rowing boat away from the shingle. When he'd climbed in, he looked up to see her standing with her back to him, staring at the well.

The mist grew thicker as he rowed out onto the loch. Soon the island was lost from view and he was alone. She had proved him right. It was stupid to get attached to people. You only ended up getting hurt.

He reached the far shore, his jaw set. As he

grew closer to the mainland, he saw someone on the shoreline. Who was that?

He rowed the last few feet, dragging the boat up onto the shore before letting go, turning to see who the figure was.

"Tavish," the stranger said, pulling down his hood. "It's been a while. I thought I'd find you here."

"Quinn? Is that you?"

The druid smiled. "You're a hard man to find, you ken?"

"What are ye doing here? Have ye been looking for me?"

"Your father is awfa sick."

"What?"

"I was looking for ye. Ah ken the laird willnae let you in but ah might be able to take him news of you."

"Ah have the stone. I can get inside to see him."

"Then you should go quick. Ah dinnae ken how much time he has."

"Will ye dae something for me, Quinn? Will ye take the boat and show her what tae dae."

"You found her then? The one from the future."

"Aye, ah did. Now, she 's brought me the stone

like you knew she would. She wants to go home and I'm no going tae stop her. I understand why she's doing it. I just wish there was another way."

"And what are you going to do?"

"Forget her."

Chapter Thirteen

Lindsey couldn't believe her misfortune. She was cold, wet, hungry, and alone. What was worse she was still no closer to going home. The mist that had been spreading from the moment she woke up had long engulfed the entire island.

She was trapped in the past at the moment she most needed to go home. All she could do was relive the dream over and over again while staring at the well.

She'd been staring at it for so long her eyes were stinging. Around her, the mist swirled like a living thing. If only she could work out what to do. The answer was there somewhere in the stones, but she could not fathom it.

The dream came again unbidden into her head. She had been outside Tavish's house in the present day, not the past, walking by several cars.

Her mother was being dragged outside, tossed into the dirt by anonymous men in suits who ignored her pleas for mercy, for just a little more time.

"Mom," she cried but Rhona didn't hear her, sobbing on the ground as more men vanished inside.

She reached out toward her mother. "I'm coming. Just hold on."

She woke up with sweat pouring down her. It hadn't been a dream. It was real. She was certain of it. At once, she was outside the hut, running for the spot where Tavish had hidden the rowing boat.

It took her far too long to find it in the dark but when she finally did, she made up for lost time, rowing faster than she thought possible, racing to the island as the sun rose. She had to get home.

Last night had been one of the hardest nights of her life. She had been desperate to tell Tavish the one thing she'd kept from him. She loved him.

She had realized during the journey south but that had only made things harder for her. She couldn't stay with him. She needed her mom to know where the locket was and there was no way of doing that other than going home and telling her.

Each day that passed only made it harder. She had been stupid, falling for someone she couldn't possibly have.

Then sitting together on the shore of the loch, him trying to get her to talk. What would have been the point of telling him?

Telling Tavish she loved him would only make a difficult situation far worse for both of them. She still had to go home. Leaving him with the knowledge that she loved him would tear a hole in an already broken man. He needed healing, like her mom, not more damage from someone broken like her.

She was damage personified. She only had to look at herself as she stared down into the well. She had a man who cared about her, who'd looked after her, who'd kissed her so perfectly she'd gone weak at the knees.

And what had she done? Pushed away the only person who could give her the emotional support she needed. Not only that but she'd hurt him in the process, shoving him away, demanding he go.

It wasn't his fault she was stuck in the past. The longer she spent alone the more the truth began to break through her defenses. None of it was his fault. He'd done nothing except be kind to her.

She was upset because she was unable to help her mom and she'd taken it out on him. Well done, Lindsey. How mature.

Where had that effort got her? Had it got her home?

Nope. She was freezing cold, the mist soaking through her clothes and seeping into her bones. She was starving hungry with no food anywhere. She was no closer to cracking the secret of the well.

Best of all, she'd told him to take the rowing boat so she had no way of getting off the island. She was stuck there alone, and unless she worked out what to do to get home, she might just starve to death, the locket hidden forever and her mom homeless.

Well done again, Lindsey. First rate job.

Why did this have to happen? Why did she have to develop feelings toward him?

She looked down into the blackness inside the well. Should she jump in? Would that take her back to the present day?

Was it deep enough for a fall to be fatal if it didn't work? It would be far worse if she broke her legs in the fall but survived. Leaning down she picked up a stone and threw it down, listening hard. Nothing. Not even a distant plink of it hitting the water. Just how deep was the thing?

Behind her, she heard the splashing of water. Turning, she could see nothing but the mist. Then out of it, a shadow fell across the water. She realized a moment later that it was a rowing boat.

At first, she thought it was Tavish coming back but before she had time to shout an apology to him for how she'd spoken to him she saw it wasn't him at all.

It was an elderly man with a shock of white hair. He was wrapped up in a cloak like Tavish's and her own.

The boat reached the shore a second later. The man slid the oars inside, then stood up. He climbed out into the water before wading up toward her. His cloak dripped on the heather as he made his way to the well.

"You must be Lindsey," the man said. "My name is Quinn and I'm here to help you."

Tavish rode fast to Castle Sinclair. He prayed he would make it in time, that his father would still be alive when he got there.

Approaching the castle after so long a strange feeling washed over him. Guilt, anger, affection, all mingled with panic over whether he had taken too long to get there.

Two guards manned the gates. They were not men he knew though after so long would he recognize anyone there?

"What do ye want?" the first guard asked. "Alms are given tae beggars on Sundays only. If ye seek charity, the abbey feeds the poor. Five miles that way."

"I seek no abbey. I seek the laird of the Sinclairs."

The second guard laughed. "Do ye now? A beggar wishing to speak to our laird. Well, what might ye have to discuss with him?"

"Ah have something for him."

"And might I ask what gift you bring? Gold? A destrier perhaps? Chainmail?"

"This." Tavish leaned down to pass the velvet bag to the guard, watching as the two of them slid it open, pulling out the contents.

"The sacred stone," the first guard said, sounding shocked. "But how did ye get this?"

"Ah am Tavish Sinclair and ah retrieved the stone to end my exile as I was bid tae dae a decade before this day."

"Tavish? Is that really you?"

The second guard vanished, leaving the first to hand the stone back to Tavish.

"The stone is returned at last," the guard said. "Praise God."

"Are ye going tae let me inside?"

The gates rattled open. The guard stood aside and watched as Tavish rode into the courtyard, taking in what had changed and what remained the same. A new armory had been built against the far wall. The chapel had been expanded. It was all so different yet so familiar.

Jumping down from his horse he carried the bag into the keep, marching up the stairs to the great hall. The laird was at the far end, deep in conversation with his retinue.

"I seek the laird," Tavish called out in a loud voice.

"Deal with him," the laird said impatiently, waving at one of his retinue.

"This way," the steward said, trying to push Tavish backward.

"Is that how you treat an old friend, Andrew?"

The man stopped, blinking as he stared at Tavish, realization spreading across his face. "Tavish?" he muttered. "Is that you? You must go. They'll have you killed. You know the law."

"I have the stone."

The steward's face turned white. He almost dragged Tavish over to the laird who looked up with fury in his eyes.

"Who disturbs my plans? I have the English on the march and a steward who cannot keep beggars from my door. Take him-" He stopped dead. "Tavish?" He was already getting up, reaching for his sword when Tavish held up the stone.

"Ah bring back the sacred stone of Clan Sinclair as you bid all those years ago. Now you will free my father and bring him to the infirmary."

The laird waved at someone in the back of the room before reaching out, his eyes wide, his fingers trembling. "The stone. Ah cannae believe the stone is back where it belongs."

"I give it freely tae you," Tavish said. "The MacIntyres return it with a plea for peace. We must come together if we are tae defend the Highlands."

He pressed it into the laird's hand. "Now tell me, does my father live?"

"He lives. Go now and free him with my blessing."

Tavish turned, trying to resist running from the room. He made it down to the dungeon in time to see the door unlocked. Inside smelt strongly, the only light coming from a thin window high in the wall.

At the far end of the room there was another open door and inside that the rattling of chains. Lifting a candle from the sconce in the corridor he walked through the dungeon and into his father's cell. The servants were already unlocking Fingal's chains, shielding him from Tavish's view.

He shoved past them, reaching down for his father's hand. He tried not to let the shock show on his face, but it was not easy. The strong Highlander he knew from his childhood, the man who'd beaten the plague and carried his son to Castle Sinclair, was gone.

In his place was a will-o-the-wisp. What hair was left was white, lank, and hanging down his shoulders. His beard was ragged, his body little more than skin and bones. Sores covered his wrists and ankles from where the manacles had been removed.

"Father," Tavish said, getting an arm around him, helping him to his feet. "Ah am back."

"Tavish?" the old man said, his voice no more than a faint wheeze. "Is that you?"

"Aye, it is me."

There was barely any weight to Fingal. Tavish could easily have lifted him into his arms but the old man was determined to walk, placing one shaky foot in front of the other as they edged their way out into the open.

The servants hovered nearby, unsure what to do with themselves.

"How long has it been?" Fingal asked as they climbed the steps to the courtyard.

"Ten years, Father."

"Ten years for them to admit the truth." He almost spat the words out before breaking off as coughs wracked his body. "To banish my son so long, how could they?" He stumbled, almost falling before Tavish caught him.

"Dinnae talk. Rest, Father."

It took five minutes to reach the top of the steps. When they walked outside Fingal winced, the bright light impossible to bear after so long in the darkness. He shielded his eyes as the two of them slowly crossed the courtyard to the infirmary. The entire place came to a standstill to watch, no one saying a word.

Once inside, Tavish helped his father into the nearest bed, draping a blanket over him and watching his eyes close.

"Bring me the apothecary," Tavish said to the steward crammed into the doorway. "My father needs tending for his ailments. And find out where Lilias is hiding. It is time she tell you all the truth."

Chapter Fourteen

L indsey tried to pluck up the courage to say something. She sat on the ground, her back against the cold stone of the well. Quinn sat opposite her, a warm smile on his face.

"You should go home," Quinn said. "You've done what you needed to do."

She shook her head, getting to her feet. "I'm not going home."

"And why not? I could send you back right now. You'd be safe. All of this will soon be a distant memory, a time that belongs to nothing but the history books."

The books, she thought. That was how she could get a message to her mother. "The stone we found," she said, getting to her feet.

"What about it?"

"The clan needs it, right?"

"Aye. More than anything, they need it to bring the highlands together."

"So would they reward the person who returned it?"

His smile broadened. "Go on. You're almost there."

"The book I read, the history of the Sinclair Clan. Who wrote it?"

"It is being written as we speak. The laird has been laboring over it for years. And to answer your question, yes."

"What question? I haven't asked a question."

"You're about to."

"What if the reward for returning the stone was to be allowed to include a message in the book, a message that would be there when..."

Her mind was already whirling. Was it possible? Could it work? Could she really leave a message for her mom to read in the future? If she could, then that meant...

She jumped to her feet. "Where's Tavish?"

"On his way tae Castle Sinclair."

"I need to find him."

"Come wi' me. Ah will row us across."

She sat in the boat while Quinn rowed. The gnawing despair that been growing inside her had vanished, replaced by a single desperate hope. She could stay.

She winced as she thought of the things she'd said to Tavish when they were last together. She would have to apologize, hope he could forgive her for pushing him away.

Then? Well, then she would tell him she didn't need to go home. She already was home. If he would have her. She thought of the kiss.

Before the boat even reached the shore she was out and splashing through the water.

"Take my horse," Quinn shouted after her. "It's a lot quicker than going on foot."

"Thank you," she shouted back, reaching the piebald nag a second later. The horse looked like it was ready to collapse but as soon as she was on its back it was running with hurricane winds behind it.

She could barely hold on, gripping the horse's neck as it galloped along the grass, heading steadily south. She didn't have to guide it or stop for it to drink. It seemed to take no time at all to reach Castle Sinclair and yet it still took an eternity.

During the journey, she thought about what Quinn had said, and about what Tavish had said.

The more she thought about it, the more she realized it was a test and one she almost failed. Whatever powers had brought her back through the past, there were other powers out there too, ones that had no interest in her happiness.

That didn't matter. What mattered was she had finally stood up for herself. She could have let Quinn send her home but she didn't. She wasn't the same person who'd come back in time. She'd changed. She could only hope she'd changed enough to get into a castle full of bloodthirsty highlanders who hated the English.

Praying she wasn't too late, she breathed a sigh of relief when a castle finally came into view. "Is that it?" she asked as the horse slowed to a canter.

The beast seemed to nod its head, coming to a halt by the gates. Two guards were standing there looking in amazement at her.

"What?" she asked. "Why are you looking at me like that?"

"You're on Quinn's horse. He doesn't let anyone else ride him. Ever."

Sliding down to the ground she looked up at the beast which was already turning and heading back the way she came. "Thank you," she called after it before turning to the guards. "Is he here?"

"Who? The druid? He went out late last night."

"No, not Quinn. Tavish. Please, tell me he's here."

"Inside. Is he expecting you?"

"No, but-"

"Then we can't let you in, not with English scouts so nearby. You sound a wee bit English in fact. Hold it there."

"No," she snapped, darting between the two of them and sprinting into the courtyard, ignoring their yelled curses after her.

"Stop her!"

"Oi!"

She continued running, looking around her at the sea of people, none of them friendly. Where was he?

"Tavish," she yelled. "Have you seen Tavish?" She grabbed the nearest person by the collar. "Where is he?"

The two guards had caught up and were just reaching for her when a voice boomed out, "What's all this blether?"

Everyone froze. Even Lindsey turned to the source of the voice, finding herself looking into the eyes of a man in his mid-fifties, as wide as he was tall, wrapped in thick furs despite the warmth of the summer sun.

"An intruder," one of the guards said, grabbing hold of Lindsey by the arm.

The other also latched himself onto her. "We think she's an English spy."

"I'm no spy," Lindsey replied, fighting to free herself. "I need to see Tavish."

The enormous man beckoned her over. The guards lifted her off her feet and carried her squirming form over to him. He looked down at her without smiling. "What do you want with Tavish Sinclair?"

"I need to speak to him. Please, it won't take a moment. I beg you."

The man again examined her. "You ken, I've been laird here for thirty-six years and I've only once before seen one with eyes as honest as yours." His voice came down as he spoke until he sounded almost warm. "You'll find him in the infirmary."

She followed his pointing finger as the guards slowly relaxed their grip. As soon as she was free, she ran over to the infirmary, pushing the door open before stopping dead.

There he was, leaning over a bed, administering

drops of something into the mouth of an elderly man who had his eyes closed.

There was something around the old man's neck. A locket. "Is that-?"

Tavish turned to look at her. "The laird gave my mother's back to me. Thought it might help him recover." He got to his feet slowly. "You're looking well."

"So are you." Lindsey's heart pounded as Tavish marched over to her, wondering what he was about to say, whether he was going to send her away as she'd done to him.

Before she knew what was happening, he put his hands on her cheeks and kissed her. This time she didn't pull away.

Instead, she closed her eyes, breathing in his scent.

His hands slid down her back, drawing her body against his. The kiss deepened and her knees turned weak. If it wasn't for his grip on her she would have fallen. At last, he pulled away and she returned to earth from somewhere high in the clouds.

He smiled at her. "Ah thought ah'd lost you."

"I thought you hated me." She could still feel his lips on hers.

"Ah thought this was what ah wanted. For me father tae be free and for me to be back in ma home." He fell silent for a moment before continuing. "Ah want you, Lindsey MacMillan."

A laugh and a sob left Lindsey at the same time. She put a hand to her mouth to calm herself, looking down and taking a deep breath before speaking. "I'm sorry for what I said. I didn't mean it. I was just…I was scared."

"No, you were right, lass. You need tae look after your mother while you have one. Ah shouldnae have been so selfish, asking ye tae stay wi' me."

"It wasn't selfish. It was honest and I couldn't handle it. I'm sorry, Tavish. Can you forgive me?"

"There's no forgiving tae dae."

"You don't hate me then? I was so afraid you'd hate me."

"Hate ye? Ah love you."

Her heart soared out of her chest and into the air, she floated upward, leaving the floor until he grabbed her and kissed her again.

"I love you too," she said between embraces.

It was some time before they parted again. Tavish frowned. "But what about your mother."

"I don't need to leave here to show her where the locket is."

"What? But how, what are ye going tae dae?"

Footsteps sounded behind Lindsey. She glanced behind her in time to see a gaunt man in white robes walking in. "How is he?" the man asked.

"Lindsey, this is Robert, our apothecary." He nodded to the figure by the door. "He's still sleeping, Robert."

"That's good," the apothecary replied, nodding toward Lindsey. "Go get some rest. There's nothing you can do until he wakes up."

"Will he live?"

"Another month in the deleterious miasma of the dungeon and I'd have said no but you got him out in time. He'll recover soon enough. Now go, he needs peace. I will tend to him."

"Send for me as soon as he wakes."

"Of course."

Lindsey looked down, surprised to find her hand entwined with Tavish's. They walked out of the infirmary together.

"I want to stay," Lindsey said. "If you'll have me."

"Ah couldnae have any other. But if you have tae go, ah understand. Ah willnae stop you."

"I know and that means the world that you would say that."

"I still dinnae understand what you're going tae dae about the locket."

She told him about her idea, writing a message in the book. "I only wish there was some way of knowing if she'll get it."

"Perhaps the druid might have a suggestion about that. Where is he anyway?"

"Probably waiting for his horse to come back to him. He let me borrow it to ride here."

"Quinn let you ride his horse? Wonders never cease. Are you sure this is what you want? Tae be here with me."

"Aye," she said with a smile. "It's the only thing I want."

Chapter Fifteen

Lindsey got up from her armchair and looked out through the window. It was the same view as ever and she was yet to get used to it. Castle life going on down there as it did every single day.

Still no sign of Tavish. She sat back down, promising herself she'd wait at least ten minutes before checking again. The pile of wood shavings at her feet grew taller. In her hands was the figure she'd been carving since he left. She wanted to get it finished before he got back, a gift to thank him for everything he'd done for her.

The horn blew just as she was getting to her feet again to look out the window. Two blasts. That could mean only one thing.

Taking the stairs two at a time she was in the courtyard before the gates were open, craning her neck to observe the returning party.

There was the laird, as big as ever, his huge warhorse the only beast capable of bearing his weight. He was laughing and slapping Tavish on the back as they rode in together.

She ran through the crowd, reaching her husband in time to see him climbing down from his horse.

"Lindsey!" he said, sweeping her into his arms and holding her tight. "Ah've missed thee something wicked."

"Did you find her?"

"Aye, we did."

"And?"

"And we were lucky not to be attacked. The laird told me everything that's been happening in the war since my exile. You must be ma lucky charm. Berwick's been sacked and Edward's close to taking Stirling again."

"We can talk about all that later. What happened with Lilias? Did she confess?"

"Let's get inside first, lass." He took her hand, walking through the crowd and into the keep. Then it was up the stairs Lindsey had come to know so well.

Past the great hall, past the laird's chamber, up to the top floor where crammed in beside the dovecote was the private rooms of the laird in waiting.

"You've kept it nice while ah've been away," Tavish said, throwing his cloak onto the back of a chair.

"I've done nothing. The serving girls work hard to impress a laird in waiting. I better hope none of them catch your eye."

"There's none in this world or the next as fair as you, Lindsey. You need fear no serving girls. And what's this?" He picked up the carving.

"Your parents and mine," she replied, watching as he examined the carving closely. "Well, Quinn served as the model for my father, but you get the idea? Do you like it?"

Tavish looked up at her. "It looks beautiful. As do you."

He placed the carving back on the table before crossing to Lindsey, grabbing hold of her and kissing her in that way she had missed more than anything else while he'd been gone.

They'd been together a year, married six months, and yet still his kisses made her go weak at the knees. His hands ran down the small of her back.

"Is it time for bed yet?" he asked, cupping her buttocks gently.

"Not even close," she replied, swatting his hands away. "Your father wishes to speak to you."

Tavish groaned. "He can wait. Ah have more important matters to discuss with ma wife."

"Oh yes, like what?"

"Like whether she wants to see the finished book."

She leaped for joy. "He got it done while you were away?"

"Aye. The scribes have even produced a copy for us. It is a late wedding gift and an apology."

"An apology?" Lindsey frowned while Tavish rummaged in his bag. "What for?"

He brought out the leather-bound volume before answering. "For not believing my father and for exiling me."

"She confessed then?"

"Aye."

"Where did you find her? Was she at the nunnery?"

"Lilias? We got there just in time. The Mother Superior is sending her to work with lepers on St. Jura, the isle toward the land of the North men."

"Norway?"

"Is that what it's called in your time?"

"This is my time, Tavish."

"Aye, but ye ken what ah mean."

"Come on, get to the point. I've waited a month to hear this story."

"She couldnae live with the guilt of what she'd done, blaming me for the death of Margaret. She took herself off to the nunnery to shut herself off from the world and beg forgiveness for what she'd done. We were lucky."

"Lucky?"

"Aye. Her Mother Superior told her to beg my forgiveness when ah got there. Let me in to see her in person. You should have seen the laird's face. Two men given consent to enter a nunnery."

"I can imagine."

"She told him what really happened. Margaret went up on the roof when I rejected her and Lilias followed. The princess teetered too close to the edge and when a gust of wind caught her she started to fall. Lilias could have caught her but she didnae.

"She watched her fall tae her death, knowing she had the perfect change to get revenge on me for not loving her. Mother Superior said working in the leper colony would be the best way to atone for almost plunging the whole country into war."

Lindsey shook her head slowly. "Now everyone knows the truth."

"Aye, I return home an innocent man once again. Now do you want to look in this book or should I go deposit it in the library?"

She took the book from him and flicked through the pages. It felt surreal seeing the actual volume that had been referenced in the book she'd read before.

"This was one of the sources in the book I read about you," she said, turning the pages slowly. "The colors are stunning."

The writing had been interspersed with illustrations that were some of the finest work she'd ever seen. Toward the middle of the book, there were pages she didn't recall reading about.

She glanced up at Tavish before continuing. Did he know how much had changed?

No longer did the story of Tavish Sinclair end in mystery, his disappearance was only the start of pages of description of the good he had done for the clan. Because of him, the clans had reunited.

Lindsey stopped, reading a sentence twice. She

hadn't been mistaken. That was her name right there in black ink on vellum.

'Then Lindsey MacMillan guided Tavish Sinclair to Castle MacIntyre. There the sacred stone of Clan Sinclair was received in the spirit of friendship from the erstwhile bitter rival of the Sinclairs. With its return, the clans were bonded for all time and the defense of Scotland strengthened beyond measure in preparation to repel Edward. As a reward for all she had done, Lindsey MacMillan was given freedom by the laird of the Sinclairs to speak these words to the future and forevermore let these words shine forth for all those to read who praise God and love the Highlands as a free land for God's people below Him upon high.'

She turned the page and there it was, her message to her mother. She read it. Then she read it again. Three, four, five times. It was really there. She ran her hands over the letters, expecting them to melt away. They remained as real as the touch of Tavish's fingers on her shoulder.

"I told you I'd think of a way to get a message to your ma," Tavish said.

She looked up to see him smiling. "You thought of it, did you?"

"You might have helped."

They laughed. Taking his hand, she moved it down to the flat of her stomach, holding it there with her fingers entwined with his. "I have something to confess," she said as realization dawned on his face.

"You're not?"

She nodded. "I thought I was late when you went, but now I'm certain."

A voice interrupted them from the doorway. "What are you two looking so happy about?"

They turned to find Fingal leaning on his walking stick. While Tavish had been away he'd improved in leaps and bounds. The apothecary had worked wonders and he no longer looked like a skeleton, his skin clean, the sores healing. The only sign of his prolonged incarceration was a fading limp.

He took a step into the room. "Ah heard you were back, Tavish. The laird tells me all is well. Your record is expunged. I suppose you have much to smile about."

"Aye, Father," Tavish said. "Once he knew the truth, he signed the contract. He has no prime heir of his blood. I am to be laird as recompense for what was done to thee and me, and my children after me will inherit the title."

"Wonderful," Fingal said with a smile. "And to think you might have ended your days an outlaw if you hadn't met yon lass there."

"Aye. Though that is not why we smile." Tavish kept his hand pressed to Lindsey's stomach.

Fingal's smile broadened, his eyes growing wide. "You dinnae mean…is it true?"

Lindsey grinned. "I'm pregnant."

Fingal threw his stick away, limping over toward her and throwing his arms around them both.

"That's wonderful," he said, losing his balance almost at once and falling onto the bed. He sat up laughing. "I am to be a grandfather." His smile faded. "Your mother would have loved to see this moment." The smile returned and lit up his face. "No doubt she is watching still. Now pass me my stick or you'll be stuck with my company all day."

"Your company is most welcome, Father."

Fingal got to his feet slowly, holding out his hand for the stick. "I will not keep a man and wife from their reunion. I will see you tonight at dinner."

By the time the horn blew for the evening meal, Lindsey and Tavish were thoroughly reacquainted. They joined the rest of the clan in the great hall, sitting on the high table beside the laird who called for silence before the food was brought out.

"Some of you will already have heard," he began, his voice echoing around the candlelit walls.

"We all now know the truth of what happened on that dark day so many years ago. Lilias the flower girl did not speak the truth during the trial of Tavish, son of Fingal. Princess Margaret, may she rest in peace, was murdered at the hands of no one. Her death was naught but an accident, most tragic and the fault of none here today."

Lindsey glanced at Tavish who nodded almost imperceptibly. The laird was not sadistic in his response to finding out the truth. He was willing to show Lilias a little mercy, not mentioning that she could have caught the princess before she fell but chose not to. He continued his speech as the room listened in silence.

"Today we return with the knowledge that the man who was once an outlaw will one day become laird of Clan Sinclair. By his side, none could ask for a better wife and lady than Lindsey who, I dinnae mince my words, saved us all.

"In her name, the village of Tavistock will be rebuilt in honor of her, the sacred stone, and all good people of Clan Sinclair. I ask you now to raise your goblets and toast the man and woman who brought back the stone and ended our feud with the MacIntyres." He lifted his horn cup above his head, mead splashing over the sides. "To Tavish and

Lindsey. May they be bonded for all days, past, present, and future."

"Tavish and Lindsey," came the response from the crowd.

"Can we no eat yet?" Fingal called out. "I'm starved and you blether on like a fishwife."

The crowd gasped but the laird just roared with laughter. "Bring in the food!"

The meal began, conversation spreading around the room. Lindsey looked at her husband and then out at the inhabitants of the castle. She smiled to herself. She was truly happy and truly in love.

She had everything she had always needed and the one thing she'd never even realized she wanted. A family with her outlaw Highlander.

Epilogue

They walked the last few yards together. It felt like the right thing to do. "Do you remember when we first came here?" Tavish asked as the carriage rolled on by.

Lindsey waited until the three of them were alone before answering. "How could I forget?"

"I want tae see the hoose!"

Tavish looked down at his son who was straining to run forward.

"Go on then," he replied with a laugh, letting go of his hand.

Thomas was off like a shot, dashing across the grass and pushing open the door to Tavish's old house. They watched him go.

"When did he get so big?" Lindsey asked. "It

doesn't seem like two minutes since he learned to walk."

"It's getting him to slow down that's the problem," Tavish replied. "I cannae keep up with him half the time."

"You do all right." She reached up and kissed his cheek before the two of them followed Thomas inside.

The house was finished. In the three years since Thomas had been born it had been completely refurbished. No longer the empty weed-strewn building Tavish remembered, it looked much like it had during his childhood.

He glanced into the main living space, unable to keep the smile from his face. "I'm going to like living here."

"Me too," Thomas said, appearing at the top of the stairs. "Which one is ma room?"

"We thought you'd be sleeping outside in the stable," Tavish replied.

Thomas stuck his tongue out before starting to giggle as his parents ran up the stairs after him. Lindsey stopped halfway, putting her hand on her stomach and wincing.

"Are you all right?" Tavish said, looking back down at her. "Is it coming?"

"At five months? I should hope not. I just need to remember I cannae run anymore."

"You're starting to sound a wee bit Scottish, ye ken?"

"Och, get away with your blether. Now where's that boy of ours, I believe he needs tickling."

A rewarding shriek was heard as the bairn hid from view in the bedroom, poking his head out from behind the curtain. Tavish scooped him into his arms and collapsed on the bed with him, Lindsey joining them a second later.

"What do you think about having a little brother or sister?" she asked. "Think you'll want to share a room with them?"

"Aye, then ah can teach them how to use a sword."

Tavish laughed. "It might be a few years before they're ready for that. Now, come on. We can't stay here all day. There are people waiting for us in Tavistock."

They headed downstairs together, making their way outside into the sunshine. Tavish glanced back at the house as they walked away.

It was finally done. There were times when it felt like it would never be finished but the craftsmen had worked hard, putting as much effort into renovating as they had into rebuilding the village.

They crested the hill and looked down. It was different again to the last time he paid a visit.

The charred earth was gone. Three years had seen lush grass grow where once was scorched nothing. The ruined buildings were gone, new ones going up fast. Another year and the place would be finished.

Surrounding the village were enclosures of cattle and sheep, past them strip fields of wheat, peas, and oats. It filled his heart to see it.

"None of this would have happened without you," he said, taking Lindsey in his arms while Thomas ran on ahead to Fingal who was waving from the village green.

"I didn't do anything much."

"Apart from get the sacred stone back and bring peace to the Highlands so we dinnae need to worry about being attacked. Other than that, you did nothing at all."

"Are you two coming?" Fingal shouted, lifting Thomas into his arms and kissing his forehead. "The laird of the MacIntyres gets here on time after a week's journey and yet you manage to be late. Come on, everyone's waiting."

"I'm surprised he didn't tell you it'll have to be different after you're laird," Lindsey said.

"I know. This morning he said it was because my baldric was twisted. I dinnae ken he's any happier than when he's cursing me for not taking this laird thing seriously enough."

"He's just worried for your people."

"Aye, I ken. He wants the clan to like me."

"They already do. Come on, before he has a heart attack."

Tavish slipped his hand into Lindsey's and together they walked through the village. At the entrance of the chapel they stopped. Fingal had already taken Thomas inside.

The porch was held up by two tall columns of stone. Onto each Celtic symbols swirled and shifted like real things, coalescing in the lintel where an intricate S symbol had been carved. "You got it finished in time then," Tavish said. "I wasnae sure ye would."

"You think a little thing like being pregnant would stop me finishing that?" she replied. "Shame on you."

"The apprentices helped, didn't they?"

"Maybe a little bit but that S is all me."

"I can tell. It looks perfect."

They walked inside to find the place packed. The MacIntyres were over to the left, their laird talking to the laird of Clan Sinclair, the two of them laughing together. Beside them, Merida looking as well as any bairn, her parents glowing with life as they doted over her.

Billy, Jock, and Matthew nodded to Tavish as Quinn moved to stand before the altar. He held up a hand. "If you wouldnae mind looking this way." The place gradually fell silent.

"Today we all come together to rededicate this chapel as a place of worship and peace."

Tavish glanced past Quinn at the alcove underneath the window. There were the dried bluebells Lindsey had gathered what seemed like a lifetime ago.

In the middle of the circle of flowers was the carving she'd done for him, the one that told him what he already knew, she was the right woman for him, the only woman for him in fact.

He tuned back into Quinn's speech in time to hear the dedication. "This church is named for Princess Margaret, may she rest in peace. The sacred stone resides here in the center of the altar as God's love resides in the center of all our hearts this day. God's love will protect the chapel of

Princess Margaret, the village of Tavistock, the clan of Sinclair and…"

Thomas suddenly crashed into his leg. He swooped the bairn into his arms, laughing as he did so. "And the future."

Everyone cheered and Thomas waved, not sure why they were all cheering him but loving the attention.

As the crowd filed outside the chapel, Tavish and Lindsey waited. The laird of the MacIntyres solemnly shook both their hands as he passed before leaving them alone with Quinn and Thomas.

"This one will be trouble," Quinn said, setting Thomas back on his feet. "You'll have your work cut out with him."

"You mean you will," Tavish replied. "If you're going to tutor him, you better get used to that energy."

"Want to play?" Thomas asked, tugging at Quinn's hand and trying to pull him outside. "I can roll twice backward without getting dizzy."

"Come on," Lindsey said, "Show me that tree you like climbing." She walked outside with him. Tavish watched them go, unable to stop smiling.

"It is good to see you happy," Quinn said. "Is she well?"

"Aye," Tavish replied. "Though she wonders about her mother sometimes."

"No doubt she does. Has she any doubts about staying?"

"No, nothing like that. She just wishes she could find out if her mom uncovered the locket."

"The Highlands have ways of helping those who wish hard enough," Quinn said, walking down the aisle to the chapel door. "Are you coming?"

"In a moment," Tavish replied. When he was alone, he walked behind the altar to the carving, pressing his finger to the figurine. "I think you would have liked her," he said quietly. "I hope you are at peace, mother."

Turning, he headed outside, finding Lindsey sitting on the grass while Thomas clambered over the low branches of the one tree that survived the fire, an old oak that he had climbed in just the same way when he was little.

He settled on the grass with his wife and together they enjoyed the last of the afternoon sun while the feast was prepared at the long tables over at the far end of the village green.

The meal took most of the day to eat and by the evening Tavish was full to bursting. He walked back with Lindsey and Thomas to their house, putting their son to bed for the first time in the room where he'd grown up.

It felt odd seeing him settle in the spot he had grown up but it also felt right, like it could not be any other way.

Lindsey was asleep soon after, Tavish lying beside her and waiting for sleep to come. When he did, he was surprised by his dream. He was outside the house, but it was different.

There was a strange carriage beside the door, but he barely had a chance to look at it before he was swept inside. There was someone inside, but it wasn't Lindsey. She was next to him, appearing out of nowhere.

Taking her hand he walked into the living room and there was a woman with gray hair and a bright red cardigan sitting beside the fireplace.

In her lap, Thomas was sitting playing with a carved wooden doll.

"I've been waiting for you," the woman said. "Your son is beautiful." Mist began swirling in through the window, surrounding the woman, swallowing her ankles. "Is this your husband?"

"Aye," Lindsey said. "Mom, I love you. I'm sorry I didn't-"

Her mom interrupted. "I love you too and

you've nothing to be sorry for." She looked sorrowfully down at the mist shifting up her calves. "There isn't much time. Go, live your life. I'm glad you found happiness with such a good man."

"Mom," Lindsey continued, trying to push the mist away that grew thicker, obscuring her from Tavish's view. "I hid the locket. Did you find it? I was so worried you'd been thrown out."

"What's your son's name?" The voice came through thick fog. Tavish could see nothing, the mist had already swallowed him up.

"He's called Thomas," he said, not sure if she heard him and then he was sitting upright in bed. He turned, surprised to find Lindsey was not only awake but in tears.

"What's the matter?" he asked. "Are you all right?"

"I dreamed about my mom," she replied. "She was right here."

"Or maybe we were there," he said, taking her in his arms.

"We? Did you? You can't have dreamed the same thing. That's impossible."

"She was downstairs with Thomas in her lap, right?"

She looked at him in the darkness, a frown spreading across her face. "But how?"

"I think Quinn might have had something to do with it. Come, settle with me."

"Do you think I'll ever see her again?"

"I have no doubt you will but not yet, not unless you want to go back home after all."

"I told you before, I am home. This is my home, here with you."

"You're happy then?"

She kissed his cheek, nestling into the crook of his arm. "I have a perfect husband and-"

A loud belch from the next bedroom echoed loudly.

Lindsey stifled a laugh. "And an almost perfect son who might perhaps have eaten a bit too much at dinner."

Tavish let his eyes close. He could smell Lindsey's delectable scent in the darkness and there was no finer perfume in the entire world.

Soon they were both asleep once more and then the only sound was that of an owl hooting on the roof above them. It spotted a mouse in the distance and, with a flap of enormous white wings, it took off in pursuit, vanishing into the darkness.

The End

What did Lindsey write in The History of the Sinclairs?
Did Rhona ever find the hidden locket?

Sign up for my newsletter and you'll get the answers in a free and exclusive bonus epilogue.

.

Sign up here.

Afterword

This story is based on the period 1290-1300, a tumultuous time in Scotland, although Tavish learned little of what was happening while he was in exile.

King Alexander of Norway, ruler of Scotland, died in 1286, having outlived his children. His granddaughter , Margaret, became heir to the Scottish throne aged three, traveling to Scotland aged seven. (I used artistic licence to adjust her age to make it better fit the timeline of story.)

Alexander had arranged in advance for Margaret to marry Edward of Caernarvon, son of Edward I, King of England. The plan was for Margaret to become Queen and Edward King once his father died, unifying England and Scotland.

Sadly, Margaret died shortly after arriving in the Orkney Islands from side effects of sea-sickness. (Or perhaps falling from a castle roof?) Her death in 1290 left a power vacuum with many nobles fighting it out to claim the Scottish throne.

In 1291 the King of England was asked to help choose who should be crowned King of Scotland. Edward was cunning, refusing to pick until the Scottish nobles swore fealty to him. On the 11th of June 1291 all Scottish castles were placed under his control. All officials were made to resign to be reappointed by him.

On 17th November 1292 he chose between Robert the Bruce and John Balliol, picking Balliol to be King of Scotland, subservient to the English crown.

When Edward ordered Balliol to provide him with troops for a planned invasion of France two years later, Balliol refused. Edward was incensed, ordering Balliol to relinquish control of his castles.

Balliol refused again, drawing an army to his side, calling on all Scots to stand up to the English at last. Several lairds refused to join him, including Robert the Bruce, a rival for the throne who assisted the English, at least at first.

In 1296, war began with Edward's men sacking Berwick-on-Tweed.

In 1297 William Wallace grew to fame for killing the English sheriff of Lanark, the event rallying more men to the Scottish cause. Robert the Bruce was sent by Edward to put them down but as he traveled north he thought hard about where his loyalties lied, eventually rejoining the Scottish side.

The English gradually worked their way north nonetheless, subduing one castle after another at a high cost in lives until in 1302 Robert the Bruce and other nobles submitted to Edward leading to a nine month truce.

In 1305 Wallace was caught and executed, and then Robert the Bruce started out on the journey that would end with him avenging Wallace's death and finally being crowned King of Scotland, ruler of a country independent from England. But that's another story!

Also by Blanche Dabney

Held by the Highlander

(Highlander's Time – Book 1)

The middle ages were a long time ago. And just around the corner.

When Beth Dagless is thrown back through time to medieval Scotland, all she wants is to find a way home. But when she's captured by a handsome Highlander straight out of the history books, she realizes going home might not be as simple as she thought.

Andrew MacIntye is a laird under siege. With rival clans massing against him, the last thing he needs is for some strange woman to appear out of nowhere, talking nonsense about traveling through time. But not only can she prove she's from the future, she's making him feel something he's never felt before, overwhelming desire.

He knows the best way to keep her safe is to get her back to her own time but how can he do that when being apart from her is agony? Little does he know that the answer to his dilemma may lie in the same magic that brought the two of them together, a magic that has one final move to make in this spellbinding game of hearts and souls.

Get your copy here

Promised to the Highlander

(Highlander's Time – Book 2)

She's running late for her wedding. Eight hundred years late.

When Kerry Sutherland falls from a window she lands with a bump in medieval Scotland. Mistaken for the fiancée of the laird's son, she's brought before the man she's supposed to marry, a rugged Highlander with arms like tree trunks and eyes that stare straight into her soul.

Callum is the courageous leader of a brutal band of Highland warriors. Betrothed to a woman he's never met, his only desire is to make sure the arranged wedding never happens. Then a beautiful stranger appears from nowhere and his entire world changes.

The more time Callum spends with Kerry, the more certain he becomes that she's his soulmate. But when his past catches up with him he's forced into an impossible choice. Marry the woman his parents picked out for him and end years of clan warfare or risk everything to be with the broken woman who's taught him the meaning of true love.

Get your copy here

Connect with Blanche

Join my mailing list here.
(Get a free bonus epilogue in return for signing up)

Follow me on Bookbub.
Like me on Facebook.
Follow me on Instagram.
Get in touch here.

Also by the Same Author

The Medieval Highlander Trilogy

Highlander's Voyage (Book 1)

Highlander's Revenge (Book 2)

Highlander's Battle (Book 3)

Highlander's Time Series

Held by the Highlander (Book 1)

Janet's Tale (Book 1.5)

Promised to the Highlander (Book 2)

Outlaw Highlander (Book 3)

Rhona's Tale (Book 3.5)

Made in the USA
Middletown, DE
28 February 2019